exile and the heart

Movement -> mapping
across
difficult   physical,
terrain   political,
Df identity   emotional,
                    etc.

exile
and
the
heart

lesbian
fiction

by

Tamai Kobayashi

women's
PRESS

CANADIAN CATALOGUING IN PUBLICATION DATA
Kobayashi, Tamai, 1965-
        Exile and the heart: lesbian fiction

ISBN 0-88961-229-3
1. Lesbians — Fiction. I. Title.

PS8571.O33E94 1998   C813'.54   C98-931792-7
PR9199.3.K62E94 1998

Cover art: Kyo Maclear
Cover design: Denise Maxwell
Editor: Sharron Proulx-Turner
Copy editor: Ann Decter
Interior design and layout: Heather Guylar
Author photograph: Hiromi Goto

The passage "Crows" from *The Hiroshima Murals: The Art of Iri Maruki and Toshi Maruki*, edited by John W. Dower and John Junkerman (Tokyo and New York: Kodansha International through Harper and Row, 1985), has been reprinted with permission of the Maruki Gallery in Japan.

Note: Clara's line on page 57 is from P. Neruda's "Puedo Escribir Los Versos . . ." and on page 60 from O. R. Castillo's "Frente La Balance, Mañana."

Published by Women's Press, Suite 302, 517 College Street, Toronto, Ontario, Canada M6G 4A2.

Women's Press acknowledges the support received for its publishing program from the Ontario Arts Council and the Canada Council for the Arts.

Printed and bound Canada.
1 2 3 4 5   2002 2001 2000 1999 1998

THE CANADA COUNCIL | LE CONSEIL DES ARTS
FOR THE ARTS | DU CANADA
SINCE 1957 | DEPUIS 1957

for h.g.

Acknowledgments

A great thanks to my editor Sharron Proulx-Turner who gently nudged me along this strange process, for her support and encouragement. For Women's Press, and their patience with a lifelong procrastinator. Thanks to my friends and communities — and here they come:

In Calgary: Hiromi, Koji, Sae, Aruna, Ashok, Larissa, *absinthe*, and Fiction Writing I and II at the University of Calgary.

In Toronto: Kyo (who also created the wonderful cover), Mona, Linda, Renee, Sil, Kristyn, Gerry (in Montreal), my parents and Satoi and Toshi, the once ALOT and basketball group, Asian ReVisions and a whole lot of people who'd fill a phone book.

Thanks to the Powell Street Festival in Vancouver, and Haruko Okano for the NAJC conference in Montreal.

Thanks to the Toronto Arts Council, Ontario Arts Council and the Canada Council for their financial support.

Wind

Kathy Nakashima glances down, pushes back her hair as it falls, lines wavering on the accordion map. She is navigator, restless, fidgeting with the radio waves: static, silence, electric hum. The car buzzes with heat and bodies, a sheen of sweat, salt-bitter against the tongue. Jan drives, her arm resting on the open window, pointing out the creeks, dugouts, sloughs, the prairie antelope and beefalo. Really? Kathy gazes along the line of horizon, thinking of the song, buffalo roaming soldiers, the deer and the antelope play, thinks of a childhood of cowboys and indians, John Wayne and Green Berets. The land streams by like a newsreel. A river, cutting deep, a falling off — of something.

They've passed through semi-desert. The deadlands, Kathy says but Jan corrects her: badlands. Hoodoos with their flat-capped tops, and the silver glint of sage. Jan, behind her shades, keeps her eyes on the road. She knows this place. Or so it seems. The dust-brown Ford shudders and coughs. Dry, altitude, a different pressure. The land has not stopped in four days.

Wind too, a constant, a sign reading Lethbridge to her eyes. Almost there, Kathy sighs. Even though it means so little. A circle on a paper. Her grandfather's grave. Kathy sticks her hand out the window, a fist, and then an open palm. To catch the breeze, to shoot it. A floating sheet of canola, luminous yellow, the roadside fruit stands of translucent gooseberry, pebbled saskatoons. They've passed the Okotoks erratics, and Kathy's wonder, how stones can be travellers, and yet they are. Abandonment, in glacial tide. Jan murmurs, soon there'll be Taber corn, and pushes back her tangled hair. Kathy gazes at her, her slope of nose, ridge of mouth, wets lips at the memory of kisses, a geography of the heart. The landscape pulls her away, away. West, the mountains, river bottoms pushed to sky, igneous, sedimentary, faultlines, erosion. Limestone, the crush of shells, eddies and tides. Kathy sleeps as the land rolls beside her. A gust shakes the car, tears in her eyes. Kathy blinks. The wind is strong in southern alberta. Dust devils. Tumbleweed. Old man coulee.

Don't, Jan shakes her head at Kathy's hand, dangling out the window. Jan drives, dreamless, looking forward. Her words, when she speaks, hold spaces around them, the distance does not fall away. Four days she has chosen motels full of buffalo heads and bibles, lamps bolted to tables, bumperstickers proclaiming *Jesus Saves*. In Winnipeg, the clerk asked, Lalonde, isn't that a Quebec name. No, she said, Metis. In Regina, they're asked if they were sisters.

Kathy gazes at Jan's face. They have passed through Blackfoot, Blood, Peigan, place names of Cypress Hills, Battleford and Buffalo Jump. What must it be like for her, Kathy wonders, these signposts, this road, that coulee, this river.

Then the bridges in Lethbridge, the high railway trestle, the line between two dots. Kathy thinks of the small towns along the way, gophers tails swinging between fence posts — cow tipping and beer — shakes herself out of cliches. Her grandfather, fisherman, how did he end here, a sky of blue, so far from shore? Or is desert another kind of ocean? Antediluvian, ice age, the inland sea. History runs you down. The car rumbles over potholes, texas gates, spitting up rocks that were once mountains. Dragons roamed here, a long time ago. There are bones to prove it.

Jan leans on the concrete pillar by the parking lot of Dixie's Motel Inn. At the centre of the lot lies the outdoor pool, promised in neon as the *utd or poo*, and behind her there is a corridor of pale blue doors, aquamarine. Jan's number is 67, her key looped onto a *Reform Party: a vote for the family* tag. At Dixie's Motel Inn there are only twenty-five rooms. Jan has counted.

Jan watches as Kathy backflips into the pool, that floating moment before the pull of earth. Jan jingles the keys in her pocket, jackknife, nickels and dimes. The air is cool as the night settles the wind across the fields. Jan murmurs, as she watches the movement across water, she must be cold, she must be freezing. Jan can feel the goosebumps on her arms, the slightest tremor of her chest. She gazes, thinking, she must love the motion, fluid, a different gravity, her body pushing through liquid, elemental. H_2 Oh.

Their cupboard-sized room smells faintly of lemon cleanser and burnt mushrooms. Painted sunflowers slump over the headboard, which holds the New Testament, the Book of Mormon, a fraying Reader's Digest. Jan ruffles through her magazines. She is between books but reads and reads and reads. Jan gathers facts like some gather diamonds, with her handful of Blackfoot and fistful of Cree. She picks up her textbook, *Land Claims in Canadian Law*, her fingers running beneath the line, the words, another landscape.

Kathy calls from the doorway, wrapped in a fuzzy blue towel. Her damp hair falls from her shoulders, droplets holding the light. The glow from the room catches her, her skin, the colour of sandalwood, of morning leaves turning to the sun. She beckons and points up to the darkness, a deep untroubled blue. There are pin-pricks in the sky.

Look, falling stars.

Meteors, Jan corrects her. They burn up in the atmosphere. Stars don't fall, they burn. Explode, go nova. Or they eat themselves alive, black holes, sucking in the light.

No, Kathy says, the vowel drawn out like a slide trombone, they're shooting stars. There — a tail, like comets.

Jan smiles. You want everything to last forever.

Kathy folds her clothes, hangs her bathing suit on the shower head, a limp and heavy green; the towel lies on the floor, forgotten. As she moves through air, another fluid, her gestures are languid, her body held simply, as herself. On the bed Jan pushes back the covers to welcoming sheets, the cool solace of layers. Kathy smiles, and dives, a falling into — something.

At the roadside Smitty's they eat the all-day breakfast, Jan, the bacon, and Kathy, the rubbery eggs. Poached like eyeballs, Jan laughs. They drive up the coulee, serpentine. By the high trestle they place their quarters, nickels, dimes, and sit back as the train rolls, long, with a red caboose, flattening their coins to a smooth oval gleam. At noon, they drive to the cemetery.

At the gravesite, Kathy stands by the name Watanabe carved in stone. Akira, her mother's father. Her hands shake as she places her gift of irises, edges of blue bleeding into white. She tries to remember her mother's instructions, fumbles with the matches — *before or after prayer* — incense, offerings to the gods. *Namu ami dabutsu.* Is it blasphemy when you don't believe? The papers rustle as she splashes the water on the headstone. Hopeless, she thinks, we're christians anyway, christians since the war. She takes the papers. It is the letter of apology, of Redress, signed by Weiner and Mulroney. Kathy strikes the match, which flickers, then devours.

She steps back. The papers blacken, curl. Touch and the papers crumble, trace on her fingertips, like the imprint of the finest sand. The wind whirls the ashes above her head, over the river.

Kathy stumbles. Gone so fast, she wonders, everything so fast.

Sharp, a train whistle, cutting.

Kathy feels the wind caressing cottonwood leaves, the stir of dust, the flight of seeds, insectal flutter of wings. The air is close, close; the sun, pushing down on her shoulders. Everything she touches clings: this place does not let you go. Even in wind, the air shudders.

She closes the door. Rolls up her window.

Are you okay? Jan tap, taps the glass.

Jan's cigarette dangles, burns holes in her eyes. Sun spots, Kathy shivers, ozone.

Yeah. Let's just get out of here.

Jan frowns. Wait, she says.

They follow the Old Man river, out of the sloping coulee, out to the highway, half an hour and turn in again to the dirt roads, dust and gravel. A clump of cottonwoods and bush and Jan stops, pushing herself from the car. She holds out her hand.

Over the ridge, the river, blue-green, and above, the Old Man Dam.

Kathy looks up. Hawks, she thinks, and sky.

The Peigan fought and fought, Jan says, and the government built the damn thing anyway. Ten years time, the silt'll be up and it'll be useless.

The stones skip, plop, plop, across the surface. Ripple, sigh, or wind.

Jan smiles.

Kathy's laughter floats, as she reaches, her fingertips stroking from hand as she rushes to the water, a leap, and surface broken, as Jan watches, a snaking envy, how easily she trusts the river to hold her.

Jan slowly pulls off her shoes, her pants, flap of shirt against the breeze. Shock of water cold, mountain run-off, the sand between her toes. She rolls against the current, hand brushing clay river bottom, push away. Farther out Kathy splashes, squeals, turns, buoyant in the water. Kathy looks at the dam, the massive concrete, thinks of the buried town of Frank, the shrug of mountain. We're downstream, she asks, can they flood us?

No, Jan shakes her head, too dry. Look. At the grass, the trees.

Kathy looks to the riverside, yellow grasses, stunted bush. Above them the hawk spirals, lifting in another current.

Lying on the riverside, the groove of her hip resting on stone, Kathy asks, why is the water so blue, blue and green, at the same time?

Limestone, Jan explains, tugging grass from a crevice, limestone dissolves in water and the river carries it. Light reflects the limestone in the water. Blue and green.

hm

Jan peels the blade from the stem, holds it between her thumbs and blows. Smiles. Leans forward. Why didn't your mother come? Why now?

Kathy glances at a dragonfly, poised by the river. Eyes blue as diamonds. She sighs. I asked her that, you know, when the letter came. You know what she said? She said, can't go home again. But I don't know what's home for her. Is it home for you?

Nah, Jan waves away a buzzing gnat. Just some place I passed through.

hm

Kathy lies back, gazes at the prairie sky. It's pretty here.

Yeah.

You made it sound like hell.

It was.

hm

On the riverbank the dragonflies dart like slivers of crystal. Dragonfly blue, dragonfly red.

In the car Jan leans forward, flicks the gas gauge with her finger, turns. First a pit stop. Gotta get some gas.

It is five clicks before they turn into Dan's Petro-Can. Jan flushes the bugs from the window and goes into the store as the attendant sits idly by. Kathy steps onto solid ground, axis and turn, the gravity of the situation. Sun falls, her skin burnished brown. She pulls the shades down in front of her eyes, the fields darkening.

For one moment, the wind is still. Hush.

Close your eyes.

The gas stop door slams. Jan strides, followed by an attendant, his finger pointing, jabbing "Get out of here and take your fucking squaw with you!"

Kathy turns, what? where?

But Jan is beside her, pushing her to the car, kicking dirt as they pull out of the drive. She grips the wheel as if to tear it in two.

Kathy breathless.

Bastard. Jan glares into the rearview. Fucking fucking bastard.

Kathy, the map crumbled at her feet.

Jan turns. Her hand strikes the dashboard, a flurry of dust. Shit, they can't even get it right.

Kathy sits; the air tight around her. The rushing fields, the breathless wind. Behind them, a sour gas spout, burning.

Cerulean

The daffodils hang brightly in the jar, severed, glowing in the early evening light.
Setsuko places them aside, to the table, then
desk, in seeming absent-mindedness. She
has just returned from Kaori's; the daffodils
were a gift. And Kaori had said, "Sorry, you
can't stay. Got to get dinner for the kids.
Gotta rush," and behind her the pumpkin
pie she'd just taken out of the oven, the swell
of warmth against the autumnal night.

But not for Setsuko.

So dismissed, she shuffled from the
house, the leaves above her, falling brightness: red, brown, orange, a luminous, mock-
ing yellow.

She thinks of how often she walks alone,
now that she is with Kaori. Kaori with her
separate time for the kids, her work, the
house, the chores. She has moved to this
strange city to be with her, yet being with
her often meant being apart. Strange. How
love can mean loneliness.

She has stepped from the bus, to the
train, to her street, walking through her door,
down to her basement apartment, the clump,
clump, echo of stairs.

\ 17

Personal isolation even despite 'liberation' of Partnership

important concept.

Love is not always 'liberating'; depends on circumstances

Her books fall to the floor.

Damn her, she thinks, I'll make my own fucking pie.

The can of pumpkin is on the shelf, the sugar on the table. The dough rolls clammy to the touch, but not too sticky, a dusting of floor, the heels of her palm — push, push — spreading across the cutting board. And easily, she slides the pan into the toaster oven, the slightest bow as she peers, adjusting the dial. All that's left is the wait. Easy as pie.

She puts on a kettle and sits, staring at the knots in the fake wood panelling.

Odd things come to mind. Appendix. *Gray's Anatomy*. Footnotes and marginalia.

She thinks of her ex-lover, Clara, who pastes her walls with maps of places she has been. Clara, dropping her j's and tearing pages out of dictionaries to roll her cigarettes. She thinks of Gracie, who lives in a straw-bale house in the Yukon, who writes twice a year, birthdays and New Year's. She thinks of all the garbage the climbers left on Everest, the fruit bats, *megachiroptera*, in Malaysia, driven to extinction, the life cycle of snail parasites. She thinks of her hair, strands of grey, of how people mistake her for a woman older and taller than she is, mistake her for Nancy Quan on the upper floor, second wing, in palaeontology.

Marginalia.

She walks to her bathroom, takes her glasses from her face and rubs her forehead. The mirror catches her reflection, but not her eyes. She blinks. The room is shrouded in smoke.

Not panic, but mild surprise.

In a cross between a thrash and a stroke, Setsuko waves her arms, momentarily dispelling the fog. She snatches the blackened pan from the metal trap of an oven, throws it on the table and with a brisk snap, opens the small window of the kitchenette. Slowly the smoke dissipates.

She gazes at the pie, burnt beyond salvation. It will have to go. And the daffodils, wilting in the jar.

At 7:45, Kaori Hayashi's alarm goes off. She takes a shower, dresses, throws the dirty laundry in the hamper, and by 8:00, she starts making breakfast. At that point Aiko begins to cry from her bedroom and the

toast burns. From the radio, sunny with cloudy periods. By the time
Kaori has Masao up, Aiko is changed into her day clothes and breakfast is on the table. Between the bites of buttered toast and the slosh
of orange juice, Kaori coaches Masao on his spelling quiz, as Aiko
knocks the milk from her highchair. After Aiko's second change of
clothes — and a trip back down to the laundry room — Kaori grabs
Masao's lunch box — made the night before — his school pack, her
briefcase, the bottle and diaper bag, and the pumpkin pie that she has
made for Masao's class Halloween party, and takes out gloves, hats,
boots, coats, and scarves and drapes these on herself and her two children. At 8:45 she is out of the house and in her driveway, struggling
with the car door, the bags, bundles, gloves, and pie, with Masao spelling out cat with a k, and Aiko, sitting on the wet grass and chewing on
the bright yellow leaves.

Her car keys are on the kitchen table.

Back from work, the rush of daycare, from school, then home,
Kaori takes a brief respite with a steaming cup of ocha, the kids by the
TV for their after dinner *Simpsons*, their mouths gaping, entranced,
enthralled. Kaori gazes at them, their faces bathed in the electronic
glow. Today she has rattled and snapped. But tomorrow, and tomorrow... She shakes her head and pushes back her bluntly cut hair, sighing. Always too late and never enough, her elision of motherhood and
sainthood: Our Lady of the Perpetually Guilty, the Kitchen of the
Immaculate Intention. She swallows her ocha, burning.

Later, as she turns to her bed, she thinks about Setsu. She checks
the answering machine, but no, nothing, and thinks, iceberg,
nine-tenths below surface, then, Titanic, and shivers. Yawning, she
crawls under her quilt, folds her sharp hands against her ribs.

Tomorrow Setsuko will come. Kaori turns, a stitch in her side.
The light is blue in darkness, cerulean. The shadows play like butterflies against the walls. Why, she wonders, why do people fall together?

She arches, struggling into sleep.

Across the city, in a separate bed, Setsuko dreams. She dreams
sea turtles, jellyfish, and anemones, molluscs peering from encrusted
shells and the strangled cry of whales. She dreams of tides and seas of
sand and continents adrift. She dreams below the coral, beyond the
ridge. She dreams and sleeps, and sleeps and dreams, her breath falling with the depths. She sleeps. Dreaming an ocean of creatures lost
and sounding.

TITANIC → (going Down /
SEX. Sinking.

A sharp swoosh of the doors and she is off the Coach Hill bus, a fistful of conciliatory daisies in her hand. Up the hill, over the fallen leaves, the abandoned husks of beetles and the stiffening shell of bees, to the house, the walkway, the door. She pauses by the window, the fog on her lips frosting on the pane and inside Kaori and the kids, the scattering mess of daycare, school and Kaori's spreadsheets across the living room floor.

She rings the bell. She hears the clatter of small children, squeals, and Kaori's caution — "Don't open the door to strangers."

The letter slot opens. Masao peers out. "It's Setsuko," he giggles.

She steps into the pull of light and warmth, but with the first step her glasses fog, turning the room into mist, sharpened by the smell of steaming rice and sizzling tonkatsu. She shrugs off her coat, toes wriggling free of boots, her shoulders unburdened. The wretchedness of the day creeps up to her and with a sigh, she throws it off. She gives a crooked smile for Kaori, a hug each for the kids.

Kaori looks at her askance.

She steps back.

But Kaori is smiling, shaking her head. "Your hands — "

Setsuko holds out her hands, palms up, like a gift or a supplication, and there they are: her white archival gloves. She must have worn them all through the drive, the corridor, the subterranean tunnel of the archives. As she strips off the gauze, she murmurs, "Hm. I didn't even know I had them on."

white/innocence [handwritten marginal note]

Five minutes later Kaori is still shaking, a gurgling laughter. Setsuko tilting her head and Masao, looking between them.

After dinner, the kids in bed after a bath and brushing teeth, Kaori and Setsuko sit in the kitchen over their cups of ocha. Dishes, washed, dried, stacked in the cupboards. Pencils cleared, lunches packed, lights dim after the last ultimatum.

Kaori's finger traces the rim of her cup: "I know we've brought this up before, but maybe we should reconsider it."

Setsu takes a long sip, holding.

"I mean, you'd be closer. And I could use some help with the kids. Makes sense, money-wise.... And we'd see each other more, without rushing around our schedules. We could set up the guest room as a study and the bus route's not that bad."

But Setsuko is shaking her head. "No. It's too far from the museum." She sets the cup between them. "Maybe we should take it slowly. So we can settle. With my job, the kids, each other."

They leave it at that.

As they turn to sleep, Setsuko curls in the bed, her eyes half-closed like a mole. Kaori runs her bath, slipping into the enveloping warmth, her ears below the surface. She listens to the creakings of the house, translated through water. Sound waves, she thinks, her eyes tracing *death* the light refractions. She rolls, and the liquid rolls with her. She thinks *from* of icebergs, broken and drifting, blue, like a bruise beneath the skin. *the unknown*

Returning to the bedroom, Kaori closes the door sharply but Setsuko does not stir. She sits on the edge, pulling back the covers, thinking, this is how the bed will remember us, our separate imprints, *Underneath* this embrace. Setsuko's breath rises and falls. Kaori closes her eyes, opens them. Blue, she thinks. Cerulean.

White innocence — Blanket effect / Theory

Setsuko wakes to the slanting fall of light through the window. She can see the brightness of newly fallen snow, the crystalline pattern of ice on the pane. Beside her, Kaori sleeps uneasily, her eyebrows furrowed. Strange, Setsuko thinks, how in sleep we carry our demons. And she's been so tired, so tired. She brushes back the tangled hair. Kaori stirs, her lips parted, a whisper, and Setsuko slips closer, a caress of hand, a stroking thigh. In sleep, Kaori turns away. The light glances brighter in the shifting day. Setsuko stands and walks to the washroom. In the living room she gazes out the window: drifts, shadows of the palest blue, and a blinding reflection of sky. The house is still, quiet. She shakes off her heaviness, steps into her clothes, jacket, scarf, out of the house, to the park below.

She walks down the hill to Edworthy, through the twisting ravine. At the bottom of the hill, she crosses the railroad tracks, Brickburn, makes her way to the bridge. She stops. A mist rises over the river, the cold air condensing above the warmer water. It seems a miracle, the light, the mist, the rushing stream. She shakes her head, staring around her. As she turns back towards the ravine she sees a young man throwing snowballs in the air, his dog chasing, chasing. His thinness, soft features, the red scarf. He looks like Michael, she realizes, blinking against the light. She hadn't thought of Michael for a long time, recalls the last time she had seen him. He looked ill, but she was used to that, his cycle of getting sick, getting well, getting sick. Sometimes she'd see him in a wheelchair, then later, walking down Church street, then in hospital, never thinking that one day she'd never see him at all.

On the day he died, she had not been thinking of him, on an April burst of sunlight, short sleeves, and roving cyclists weaving through the streets. It had been the first real day of spring, with a burst of crocuses and dogs rambling in Withrow park and people sitting on sidewalk patio cafes. Walking home, her jacket on her arm, light falling through the slowly budding branches.

She looks towards the river. A muffled rumble, and turns. The dog runs towards her, crossing the road.

Turning, she could have missed it, but waits. And gasps as if the car struck her, breath torn from her lungs. But it is the dog, the horrible thud, bodily crush of muscle against metal, reddening muzzle, the dog, with its blood spraying breath, eyes rolling back in terror, red teeth, stiffening, movement of limbs through air, moving with the cry of the man, a clear arc of urine, shuddering release, and stillness, awful stillness and quiet of the woods.

The young man stands by the edge of the road. He is weeping. The car has driven away.

Setsuko walks to the dog. It is a beautiful greyhound, with the sleekness of body not yet fully grown. Pink speckles float on its muzzle and a leg lies at an odd, disturbing angle. She stands, staring at the animal, its spasms fading. She looks at the man, and realizes he can come no closer. The sky is far away.

She picks up the dog, surprised at how light it is, and carries it to the side of the road where he stands. Gentle steps, the crunch, crunch of snow. She holds out her arms, the dog between them, and carefully he takes the body, cradling. He is no longer weeping. She looks at his face, red scarf, liquid eyes. He looks nothing like Michael.

He turns away, a silent thanks.

Setsuko stands, smeared with blood and urine. She begins walking up the hill, but her footholds slip, break the crust of ice, of snow. Her heart pounds, she thinks, abominable, the loneliness of heights, of deep sea creatures. At the crest of the hill she runs, the air cutting her lungs, her breath, a hollow mist. She can see Kaori, with Masao and Aiko in front of the house, looking like islands in an ocean of

White as oppressiv

whiteness. She brushes away the wetness fr
towards them, over the road, the field, the g
they wait, across the drifting waves of snow

light = Release; final freedom from
oppression which acts as
form of sickness

A Night
at the
Edge of
the World

Kathy wakes to the light spilling in through the window, to a whisper of leaves on the sill. The light, filtering through branches and leaves, holds the room with a certain clarity in the solitary hour. Kathy rises. She casts her eyes over the overflowing bookshelves, her paper flooded desk, the posters of Pride Day, Taiko and Take Back the Night. She turns to Gen, who lies beside her, a figure of Kannon between her breasts. The scar beneath her chin glistens. Kathy strokes her thick, bristling hair but Gen turns, nuzzling deep into her pillows.

Tick tick in the mirror. A step to the stairway, a glance down the hall.

Tick

In the bathroom, she splashes her face with cold water, flicks on the light and straightens, blinking hard. Nose, mouth, eyes, the old mirror game. In her voice and gestures Kathy resembles her mother, the

Watanabe's, but from her father she carries the delicate face and hands of the Nakashima's, carefully passed down from generation to generation.

Tock

Kathy opens her palm, closes her fist. She frowns. She glances at the calendar tacked to the wall, Cezanne's blue horses. Blue. She walks back to the bedroom and gazes down at the woman sleeping peacefully, the rise and fall of breasts. Kathy closes her eyes, opens them. Across the room the mirror winks back at her. Mornings, beginnings, the day born anew. There is nothing to fear after all, after everything. The doors are locked, the sky clear, and Jizo-san stands praying by the window.

Gen can hear Kathy singing in the kitchen, her morning ritual of coffee and bagels. She stretches, a simple animal pleasure of limbs, of waking from rumpled sheets, of cool air breathing into skin. Tonight is the party, Jan's going away party. Gen rolls as she feels a fluttering loss: away. She thinks of Jan, ex of Kathy's, and wonders how far an ex goes before becoming the comfort of friend, sighing that an army of ex-lovers carry a lot of baggage. She turns, gazes at the ceiling, the pattern of stucco and spider webs. But Kathy is singing in the kitchen, the bed still warm, and Gen can smell the coffee, dark and earthy, can feel the glow of sunlight from the window, the heaviness of her body, silkiness of sheets tangled around her legs, the lightness of air hovering over her belly. Kathy's footsteps near as Gen closes her eyes, waiting

touch

and Kathy finds her, warmth along hollows of hips and thighs, a hand stroking the small of back and it is today, this morning, Gen, with the aroma of coffee in the air, bagels, buttered on the table and Kathy, singing, her body humming in time, into the beginnings of the afternoon.

Sandra Chan taps her foot. The movement jiggles her belly, as she looks down. Her arms cross her breasts. She feels old and fat as a cow.

A great farting moan from down the hall.

"Christ!"

26 /

Another bellow, low and mean.

"Shut the fuck up!" Sandy slaps the wall. "Nao!" Hand against ears, Sandy tries to push out the groans of Naomi's saxophone, squeaks and burps. As she runs down the hallway, she bangs the walls with her fists. At Nao's room, she kicks open the door.

Nao, in surprise, slips the reed out of her mouth and pulls out the dingy earplugs.

In one motion, Sandy grabs the squishy yellow plugs, tosses them out the window.

"Hey!" Nao cries, but they are gone, bouncing down the rusting eavestrough. "What's your problem?"

"My problem is you. Or more precisely, you and that damned saxophone. Now, we either stick to our agreement, or I stick that horn up your ass and around the corner!"

"San, I didn't even know you were in the house."

"I've been pounding on the walls for the last fifteen minutes!"

"Okay, okay, sorry. I had the plugs in."

"Why do use the damn things anyway? Fucking tampons for your ears."

Naomi slips her saxophone off her strap. "Don't know what you're so pissed about."

Sandy gazes at the clock. The cat's eyes tick in the corner. She turns and strides back to her room.

"Hey, hey — " Nao follows, the scuff scuff of slippers against the wooden floor.

Sandy pauses: "Veronica left this morning."

Fuck. Oh fuck. "I'm sorry Sandy."

Sandy shrugs, faces the door. "Crash'n burn. Anyway. Tonight's the party. At Kathy and Gen's, remember. I've got to go get the rum." She turns, the click of the door behind her.

Nao sets down the saxophone, sits on the floor.

"Fuck. Holy fuck."

Ana and Sharm pause before they ring the bell, their arms full with dahl and pita, a bundle of thistles and roses.

Sharmini bites her lip.

"Don't worry, I won't embarrass you in front of your friends," Ana jokes. She shifts the roses in her arms, the bowl of hummus.

Sharm laughs. "Just don't believe everything you hear, okay?"

"So Kathy is Jan's ex-lover, and you are the ex-ex of Sandy?"

"Do I have to draw you a picture?"

"It would help. Maybe a timeline. Or a graph —"

The door opens to a bustle of hugs and hellos.

"Sharmini," Kathy cries out, "how are you doing? So, you've finally brought the woman." She turns to Ana. "You'll have to take us all at once but we're pretty harmless."

"Harmless?" Sharmini shakes her head. She gazes from Kathy, tall and casually at ease, to Ana, small and observant.

Kathy smiles, sees the protective gleam in Sharmini's eye, reaches for a shaker and glasses; Sharm was always more comfortable with a drink in hand. As she pours, she can see Sharmini and Ana in a mirror's reflection, the space held between them, touch and glance of new lovers.

"Come, come," Gen waves Ana to the balcony. Her hands are wet from the spring rolls and she wipes them against her shirt. She takes the chips and dip, the tray of vegetables out to the table on the balcony, smiles at Ana, a nod hello. "It's less crowded out here."

On the balcony Ana gazes over the park; canopy of leaves, maples, oaks, poplars, shifting shades of green. "The view is very beautiful," Ana turns and sees Gen glancing at Kathy and Sharm who giggle and chatter in the living room.

"Ah, our social butterflies," Gen smiles.

Ana laughs, the lightness in her chest, rising. The sun, the wind, the afternoon. "It's good, now they can talk about us."

A knock and Kathy opens the door to Naomi, with a six-pack of beer and Sandy, a fistful of cuban rum.

"Hiya guys."

"Here's the rum. Where's Jan?" Sandy brushes by Kathy, to the living room.

"Well, hello to you too."

Naomi waves not-so-discreetly and mouths the name "Veronica."

Kathy sighs, follows Sandy into the kitchen. "Well?"

"Well what?"

"What about Veronica?"

"She's gone."

"Gone?"

"Yeah."

"Sandy, what the hell is going on?"

"I've been dumped, you idiot." Sandy pours her rum and coke. "And if you're even thinking 'I told you so,' I'll snap your head off."

Kathy rubs her forehead. "Sharmini's out there."

"Yeah, I saw her car out front."

"Her... girlfriend is with her."

"Christ. The world doesn't sit still for anyone, eh?" Sandy takes her drink, swallows in a flash. "Don't worry, I'll be alright. Besides, I wouldn't miss this for the world. Crash'n burn baby."

At twelve the doorbell peals.

Kathy opens the door and is swept up by a big, strong woman in a brown fedora. Kathy shakes her head. "You don't change, do you?"

"Neither do you."

Kathy takes her arm, "Come on in."

"Nice place," Jan nods, gazing at the posters. "Looks like you two have settled in."

"The not-so-subtle art of compromise," Kathy explains, "I listen to her enka, she trashes my Abba and we both turn on Nina Simone."

"Where is everybody?"

"Out on the balcony. Go on, I'll fix your drink."

From the living room Jan can see the women on the balcony, their faces lit by the light thrown from candles, soft, golden against the darkness. She looks at Naomi, pulling at her sax strap, and Ana, her hands casting shadows leaping against the wall. Sharm, with her eyes as bright as the flames, as dark as the sky. Below them the park is empty, it is as if they are on the edge of the world.   Isolation

Kathy steps behind her, whispers, "Go on, they've been waiting for you."

"Ten years. Ten years in the same place is a long time."

As Jan steps onto the balcony they ring in their hellos, soft hugs, hands clasping, falling away.

Kathy sets Jan's drink on the table, brushing her shoulder.

Ana's hand is on Jan's arm. "Lisa is on her overnight shift and Clara sends her regards, she wanted to make it, but she's working on

\ 29

an article against the new immigration law. She is really up to her neck in it."

"Is that the fingerprinting thing?" asks Kathy.

Ana nods. "That's one of the many nasty surprises. It is bad. They are closing the doors on the refugees, leaving us to rot."

"Welcome to Canada, home of the War Measures, Exculsion and Indian Acts," Nao toasts ironically to the sky.

Sharm raps her knuckles against the table. "Now, why are you going west?"

Jan takes a breath, pulling herself up. She looks at Sharm, at the lights that spin, dancing off her glass.

"I've been thinking about stuff, ever since I got back from the peace camp at Kanesatake. Stuff around getting back to things," she began. "I'm going to see if I can track down my sister, my younger sister." Her fingers trace the patterns on her sleeve. "I heard she was in Vancouver. And that's where I'm going. She's my only family, blood family." She glances at Kathy. "I'll take her some irises, the colour of the sea." Jan sits up, pulls off her fedora, her dark brown hair falling in waves about her face. She pulls out her keys. "I'm leaving this with you." She places the keys in Kathy's hands.

Kathy sits back.

"Half of it's yours anyways."

"Jan, I don't even drive."

"Gen does. And you can always learn."

"Yes, but — "

"That's it then." Jan raises her arms. "If I come back, you can just say you were keeping it for me."

"And if you don't?"

Jan just shrugs her shoulders.

Kathy shakes her head. "You know I can't take this."

"Kathy — "

"No."

"The art of compromise, remember?"

"You can't pull this on me."

"Christsakes," Jan rubs her forehead, "can't you take something for once in your life?"

Kathy's eyes flicker in the candlelight. Her fingers close around the keys. "Alright, Jan. Thanks."

They sit back.

"Japanese ritual," Nao explains. "You take it, no, you take it, no, you take it, no you — "

Laughter, soft, into a familiar ease.

Ana lifts her head, her eyes shining. "So mujer, you are going home?" The lilt in her voice sings into a question.

"As close as a half-breed can get, I'm going home."

Ana stands, with her glass in hand, raised in a toast. "Then to our exiles and our journeys. Ir a la montana."

They stand and toast to each other, to the edge of the sky.

Gen asks, "What does that mean, ir a montana?"

Ana gazes up into the sky, the stars. "What I mean. To go to the mountains, to move against the body of the woman you love, to go home."

"Home," Sharm murmurs.

"It is strange. There are no mountains here. A lake you cannot swim in and this poison in the sky. A country that freezes you in wintertime. And the wealth, the waste is obscene. The language is like sand in your throat and the people are cold, cold. It is like prison, waiting for the papers to come."

"I've been here all my life and they're still asking me where I'm from, how long have I been here, my English is so good," Kathy remarks.

"Or they tell you to go back where you came from," Jan adds.

Naomi looks at Sandy. "Remember the time we went into the bar on Parliament and they asked us if we knew that it was a women's bar. Jezuz. I'd been going there for ages. Music sucks, though."

"It's a surprise," Sharm reflects, "because you realize that all that time they've never seen you. Never."

"And I was in a leather jacket!"

"It isn't that they don't see you. One thing we are is visible. They ignore you. We don't suddenly disappear. Selective amnesia. It takes a lot of effort. My mom's an expert at it," Sandy explains. "She's been dying to see me married, to a Chinese man, no less. By now she'd settle for a boyfriend, any boyfriend. And there's never a word about all those women I've brought home."

"A cast of thousands," Naomi booms, ducking just in time to avoid Sandy's missile.

"Well, I'm just saying it's better to be single than to go through all that hassle," Sandy retorts.

"Mothers are very, very hard," Sharm sighs.

Gen turns to gather the empty hummus bowl, but Kathy's arm slips around and holds her.

"Kath, how's your mum doing?" Jan asks.

"She's doing alright. But I think we have this mutual antagonism thing going."

Sandy brushes back her hair, "Yeah, I know the feeling. The minute she sees me my mom gets red in the face and this shortness of breath. Could be all that yelling, though. 'Juk sing, juk sing!' But God, for someone I'm trying to avoid, I sure run into her a lot."

"Some things you never seem able to get rid of," Sharm smiles, brushing back a strand of Ana's long, entwining hair. "But I guess that's just the way it goes."

"Yes, life is like a roller coaster," Naomi muses philosophically, leans back and steeples her fingers, "and throughout its twists and turns we ride in the hope that it will be the ones behind us, and not in front of us, who barf up."

"God, that's gross," Sharm laughs in spite of herself.

"Yeah, but I have to live with her," Sandy adds, mournfully, "And that damned saxophone."

At four o'clock they hover in the hallway with their reluctant goodbyes. Sharm steps out with Ana, waving. As Sandy revs up her car for Jan and Naomi, Gen hands out the potluck rituals of Tupperware and Saran-Wrap.

Kathy stands with Jan in the hallway.

"When do you think you'll be back in town?"

"I don't know. Maybe never." Jan pushes back her hat. "Look me up when you're in BC."

Kathy nods. "You take care of yourself."

"I always do."

"Yeah, right," Kathy laughs, and Jan smiles back at her. Kathy thinks of dragonflies at the Old Man dam, the brush of cottonwoods. "I hope you find her," she adds softly.

"Yeah."

Jan sweeps her up in a big hug, swings her around. She sets her down, kisses her goodbye and with a shout she is out the door.

tick

tock

Kathy holds herself. She closes the door and turns off the light. She leans against the wall, waits for her eyes to adjust to the darkness. The room is quiet, distortion of shadows, the lateness of the hour. She looks to the balcony and sees Gen gathering glasses and bottles. She closes her eyes, unsteady. In the bedroom she stretches out on the bed, surrendering to its soft impartial embrace. By the time Gen has returned, the tears on her pillow have completely dried.

Given Names

Kathy studies the scar on Gen's left hand that carefully guides the steering wheel. Gen has small hands, with lines that are strong and fine but with that small, sharp imperfection. Kathy gazes at Gen's face, at the broad features and dark eyebrows, how they give her a certain owlish seriousness. Her spectacles, the glint of metal, wall of glass. There is a scar that runs below the line of Gen's chin; if she turns with her face slightly tilted upward, Kathy would be able to see it, a thin jagged line that could only be caught by those who were looking, those who knew.

Kathy smiles, glances in the mirror. "I think we'll be there in thirty minutes."

Gen nods.

It has been nearly three years since Kathy saw her mother, her last visit. She chews her lip, thinking there will be the same questions about her life, her job, a boyfriend. She glances down at her fingers, the closed palms. The landscape tumbles by, a dragging blur of strip malls and billboards. Palio's pizza palace has turned into a MegaVideo store and the old roller rink is long gone. There, the hydro field where she and Dennie burned down Thorton's wooden shack, playing with matches stolen from Macs, the summers of tag, spud and hide'n'seek. Even there, behind the park bushes where she had her first kiss from Sharon Kristoff in the sixth grade.

They drive up Victoria, a suburban labyrinth of crescents, drives and greens.

"It's in a little deeper," Kathy leans forward. "One seventy-five."

Gen pulls up in front of a square, squat apartment building, *Astor Place*, balcony rails bleeding rust and fading red brick. They park in front, taking their bags through the lobby and up the elevator. The hallway, a tunnel of darkness, the silence of enclosed spaces.

Kathy hesitates, raises her hand, her knuckles scrapping the wood. Luck, she thinks. Three strikes out. There is a moment in which she thinks, I could turn around and leave, just like that, and she can imagine it. She has imagined it a thousand times, her flight, her mother's arms. But her mother, opening the door, greets her with a calm smile and soft hello, as if her daughter visited every weekend, as if she had spoken to her yesterday. Norma Nakashima, her hair flecked with grey. Kathy towers over her. Between them there is little resemblance.

"Mom, this is Gen, Gen Tanaka." Kathy turns. "Gen, Norma Nakashima."

Gen bows slightly. "Hello Mrs. Nakashima."

"Yes. Kathy's roommate." She gestures towards the living room. "Come in. Are you two hungry? Would you like something to drink?"

They shake their heads and walk to the over-stuffed couch. Norma Nakashima excuses herself and returns a moment later with a tray of cakes and cookies and a pot of steaming tea. Kathy gazes at the family portraits on the bureau, the familiar scraps and scratches of the room.

"Still looks the same, Mum."

Norma Nakashima smiles. "How was the drive?"

"We stopped by the seaway last night," Kathy replies, pulling back her long black hair. "It wasn't too bad, but then, Gen did all the driving."

"Gen, you must be tired." Norma Nakashima turns to Kathy. "I think your friend should have your old room. Robbie is in Detroit, business trips, you know. His room is such a mess. You could sleep here, on the pull-out couch. Would that be alright?"

They both look at each other and nod in unison, "Yes, oh yes."

id + acceptance

Norma Nakashima rises from the couch. "I should let you two wash up and settle in."

And there she leaves them.

For dinner they have a special chicken dish that Kathy's mother prepares, an Ottawa dish, she jokes, chicken-catch-a-Tory. Kathy sits, not quite believing: her mother and lover in the same room, sitting down to dinner. They are strangers to each other, but it seems to Kathy that the intricacies of their gestures weave them into a bond akin to blood ties, family names, family honour. And Gen does look like she belongs here, at this table.

"So, tell me Gen, how did you and Kathy meet?"

"Uh. We met at ah, um, a march two years ago."

"A march?"

"It was Take Back the Night, protesting violence against women," Gen adds, "The first one after the Montreal Massacre."

Kathy's fork grates against her plate.

"Are you related to the Tanaka's of the *Nikkei Shimbun?*"

Gen shakes her head. "I'm not related to anyone."

"Are you sansei, yonsei?"

"No. I was born in Japan. Near Izu. Between the mountains and the sea."

"Ah. My father came from the south," Norma Nakashima says, "but that was before the First World War. Came here to find his fortune."

"Yes," Gen nods, "so did mine."

"Did he find it?"

"No."

Norma Nakashima sighs. "Neither did mine." She places the ocha in front of Gen, along with the tsukemono, neatly arranged in the Flintstones dish. "Everything was so hard then. My father worked near Steveston, in fishing season. He eventually got his own boat. He never did learn much English." She pours the ocha, a soft, translucent green.

"I was always my father's translator," Gen says. "It was a funny feeling, being stuck in the middle. You grow up fast swallowing a lot of insults, the stuff you don't pass on."

hmmm

Creation of Scars

\ 37

"Yes, I did grow up fast. And stuck in the middle. Trying to be Japanese for my parents and Canadian for myself."

"As if it had to be one or the other."

"Well, in those days... Kathy you're not eating."

Kathy shuffles the food on her plate.

"They tried so hard," Norma Nakashima reflects.

"And how I resented it."

"Yes, I suppose I did, too."

"Did they cart you off to Japanese school?" Gen asks.

"Every day, after school," Norma Nakashima replies with a smile. "How I hated it. That was in Vancouver, though. On Alexander Street. Of course, that was before the war. Afterwards we never went back. For a long time you couldn't."

Kathy refills their cups.

"My grandfather died in the war." Gen remembers the small lacquered box with the offering of rice cakes and burning incense, the picture above the alcove.

"My uncle died in Italy. In 1945. They sent a small box and a ribbon."

"While your family was here, in a camp?"

"Yes."

Gen reflects. "We would have been enemies then?"

"No." It is Kathy, the first words she has spoken during the entire meal.

After dinner they pull out the family photo album.

Mr. and Mrs. Nakashima in black and white. They stand stiffly against a background of impossibly neat hills and symmetrical trees, uncomfortably dignified. In John Nakashima's face you can see it; Kathy is already a possibility. The next photograph, still in black and white, is the little bundle that is Robbie. From image to image Robbie grows larger, crawling, walking, running. Then Kathy appears, with her father's eyes. She grows, along with Robbie, as Mr. and Mrs. Nakashima slip into the background. The pages go on, Robbie and Kathy getting older, their features settling into adulthood. John and Norma Nakashima grow smaller and smaller. John disappears, but there is a funeral program, faded yellow, a flower pressed between the sheets.

Kathy strokes the crumbling petals. "My father died in 1986."

Norma Nakashima turns the page. It is Robbie in his graduation gown, holding his diploma. "He's a computer programmer now," she says.

Kathy makes one last appearance. She is staring into the camera. Her hair is long and she is holding a wine glass. But it's there in the photograph. She is young, young, heartbreakingly so. And that is the end of it.

Gen looks up, puzzled. "That's it? Where are you? What happens now?"

"I drop out of university, get a dead end job, and don't get married." *expectations Lost*

Norma Nakashima closes the book and places it in the cabinet beside the fragile china and faded rosemarys. In her hands there's a slight tremor, as she brushes dust off the fresco of the bureau. She looks older than any photograph can capture.

Kathy walks into Gen's room, where she lies on the bed and stretches out beside her.

"You okay?" Gen's voice, softly.

"Yeah."

On the ceiling they can see the reflections of shadows spilling in from the window.

Kathy turns to Gen. "She's acting pretty weird."

"What do you mean?"

"That's it."

Gen, her eyebrows frowning.

"She's acting, well, normal." Kathy turns to the ceiling. "She should have asked about my damn job. Or Robbie making sixty thousand a year. Or I should be getting married. God. If he's making that much money why doesn't he grow up and move out. Or at least set her up in a better area, out of this dump. Do his own fucking laundry."

"Maybe she's changing."

"We're talking about my mother here."

Gen holds her breath for a second. "You're acting pretty weird yourself."

"Oh Gen, you don't get it."

Gen, motherless, fatherless, looks up at the ceiling, at the reflecting shadow of leaves. "No, I guess I don't."

Kathy pulls the curtains against the darkness, flicks on the table side lamp in the living room. She leans over the table, eyes intent on a photo album, this, from behind the others, unfamiliar, a faded blue, swept clean of dust.

In the photograph there is a girl standing in what seems to be a railway station. The girl is in a plain dress, with a small hat and purse in her hands, poised on the brink of adulthood. The year is 1945, written below the photograph. The girl is Norma Watanabe. She must have been fifteen-years-old.

Her mother, Kathy thinks, it must be Union Station, when she came east, after the war. Before or after Lethbridge, she wonders.

Kathy flips a page. Young Norma in bobby socks, with school friends at a party. Her hair is curled in an old-fashioned way and her dress bounces with frills. She looks happy, after all, but one can never tell with photographs.

In page after page this girl appears. A young woman really. Unfamiliar, yet . . . Kathy shakes her head. Her father appears. Stiff and charmingly shy. Then there is the wedding photograph. And oddly enough, at the end of the album, are photographs of a barracks of sorts and a shot of a row of tents.

"Slocan," Kathy whispers, as if that explained everything. She closes the album, but as she places it on the shelf something slips from beneath the cover. Curious, Kathy places it on the table. It is a child's notebook, and written in a child's hand is the name Harumi Watanabe.

Harumi Watanabe? Kathy opens the notebook. 1941. Nihon-go Gakko Picnic. There is a photograph. A child holding a doll. The edges of the photograph are charred. Harumi Watanabe. Her mother.

Close it, she tells herself, close it and walk away.

Trembling, she slips the photograph back into the album, beneath the cover, shaking as if she has felt the sigh of a ghost breathing over her shoulder, as if all that she has known were dancing in front of her in this moment of vertigo, as if the past can be held in the name of one she never knew, this child gazing into a future unimagined.

Kathy closes the album. She can hear wind and leaves, and distantly, a freight train, cry or whistle. She tumbles into the pull-out bed and falls into a restless, dreamless sleep.

Splash of oil, splatter of eggs as Kathy rattles the skillet, the light through the windows, familiar, this place, kitchen cupboards, the dent in the bathtub, a shin scarring pull-out bed. But Gen stumbles out of her room, rubs her eyes. Her hair is a bristle, cubist, all angles. She looks almost angelic.

"Hey, monshishi," Kathy teases. Gen yawns, her entire body stretching into a grimace. She stalks to the washroom and Kathy hears the shower at full blast.

Kathy shuffles the eggs, turns down the heat. Maybe she'll go to the Gallery, or wander down Sussex, into the Market. She needs a break, fresh air. Some vegetables would be nice.

She hears the pipes groan as the water is cut and Gen struggling with the bathroom mist, her cloudy specs.

Kathy turns off the heat, takes the skillet off the element. The eggs stare back at her. Mother's daughter, she thinks as she slips them onto a plate.

"Gen, I've made you some breakfast."

Curses from the bedroom.

Kathy walks to the door, watches Gen stumble as she furiously dries her hair with the towels. Mornings are a difficult time for Gen. The socks seem to conspire against her, skulking in the corners of the room, appearing in mismatched pairs. Sweaters suffocate, pants are two-legged traps. And wintertime is the worst: gloves to be lost, and all the endless zippers and buttons. Yet above it all, Gen's small round head would pop out of the shirts and sweaters, her brow stubbornly knit in concentration. Kathy reaches out, pushing back the slick, spiky hair. "Morning, maru-maru-san," she whispers as she kisses her fore-head.

Gen growls back.

"Hungry? I've made eggs. Mum's out, you know she's doing some tai chi at the community centre down the block."

They sit down to breakfast.

"I'm thinking of heading into town, taking in the Market. Do you want to come? We can play the tourist."

"I dunno. I may just take it easy."

"Lazy bones."

Gen slouches forward. "I'm getting old Kathy. I think I'm just going to veg out on the balcony, catch up on my books."

"Well, I'm going to the Market. Do you want anything?"

Gen shakes her head.

Kathy rises from the table and walks to the bed-couch. She strips the sheets and folds the bed, replacing the cushions, pushing the table into place. She strides into the washroom, getting ready for the day.

Kathy steps off the bus at Wellington. To her left are the Parliament buildings, to her right the river. She starts down the street to Sussex. Coming in, she was struck by the wealth of this city, its bureaucracy. Ministry of Such-and-Such, Department of Whatever. The streets are clean, the parks well-tended, even the lawns seem manicured. Kathy sighs. She can play the tourist for one day. She realizes that living here, she had gotten used to it. Perhaps even grown fond of it.

From the Market you can see the glass cathedral of the Gallery. She wanders among the stalls, the open tables, stopping outside of the Bagels and Buns Shop. She steps in, gets herself a coffee, cream bagel and a seat by the window. Kathy sits over her cup, closes her eyes. She can feel the steam from the coffee seep into her eyes, cling to her lashes. The coffee smells rich, like fertile earth after rain, the layer of leaves and years.

Her mother. This time there are no questions, no recriminations. At times it seems to Kathy that her mother is apologetic. And that notebook. Harumi Watanabe.

Kathy tears her bagel, rolls dough-pebbles in her hands. She shivers. Does her mother know? That she is a lesbian, that Gen is her lover? No, god, it would kill her. But something was there. Her mother had never talked to her about the Internment, never spoke about herself for that matter. And am I any different, Kathy wonders. Kathy knows she will never ask for her mother's blessing. She remembers the last time she visited. Three years ago, after her final break-up with Jan. She had run away from Toronto, taking the midnight bus home, arriving silent and exhausted, eyes red and weary. Crying into her pillows every night, pacing the floor. Her mother must have heard it, must have seen something. And Kathy, aching for a gesture that would comfort her. But it never came. She retreated into her own angry grief, returning to Toronto. Three years ago.

Kathy shakes her head. What did it matter? Water under bridges burnt long ago. She glances at her watch. Time enough to take a last glance around, to buy some groceries for tonight's dinner. She quickly swallows her coffee cold, and tosses the bagel into the trash.

Back through Elizabeth, along the canal, Kathy leans into her seat, feeling the bumps and jolts of the ride. Five o'clock. It is too much for so little time. They will be leaving tomorrow morning for the long drive home. Home. She looks out the window to the familiar streets of her childhood. Not much has changed. Even in herself. She is still the child who wept in the dark, fearful and frightfully alone.

What does she expect? To change, in two days, the patterns of the last twenty-eight years? But there is more to it, Kathy presses, if only she could figure it out.

She gets off the bus at Evans and begins making her way across the park by Palmerston High. The schoolyard is deserted. But of course, it is Sunday and school has not yet started for the fall. Palmerston. She wonders if her old locker still has that collection of bubblegum pasted on its top, or, at the back, those secret initials, K.N. loves S.K. Where would Sharon Kristoff be right now? Respectfully married? With children? Or maybe with a woman by her side and her own silent questions.

Kathy pauses in front of her mother's apartment building. What were your choices, Mum? Did you ever have someone's secret initials carved in the back of your locker? Did you ever kiss a woman behind the bushes of Belmont Park and stroke her breasts under her woollen sweater?

As Kathy steps into the elevator she meets her reflection in the mirrored wall. They were the only Japanese family for miles around. Occasionally she would see one of the Changs but she had kept clear of them. People had trouble telling them apart as it was. Kuldeep Singh had lasted only one semester at Palmerston. It was the times, Kathy tells herself. The seventies. And you, Mum? Forty years since the war.

She stops outside the door, the jangle of her keys startling her. She can hear her mother's voice floating through the living room:

"Karasu/naze naku no/karasu wa yama ni..." she breaks off. "Now how did that go..."

Gen nods. "Naze naku no. I've always wondered what that meant."

"Mukashi no uta ne."

\ 43

Kathy closes the door behind her.

"Kathy," Norma Nakashima turns to her, "how was the Market?"

"The same. What were you two doing just now?"

"Trying to remember the words to an old lullaby."

Kathy places her vegetables in the kitchen. "I never knew you spoke that well Mum."

"And look," Gen lifts the lid off the steaming pot, "udon!"

"Oh, everyone knows how to make udon," says Norma Nakashima.

Kathy looks down at her useless vegetables. "Do you need any help?"

"No, we're fine."

They sit down to dinner.

"My uncle Takao, he was one for gambling," Norma Nakashima continues, "Drinking and gambling, drinking and gambling. But what other life could he have had in a fisherman's camp, up in Skeena for such a long time. And in the sawmills it was just as bad, he lost two fingers, and even after the strike he couldn't get a 'white wage.'"

"What wage?" Gen sprinkles the togarashi into her bowl.

"Oh, Caucasians were paid more in most places. Things were different in those days. Couldn't be a doctor, or an engineer, no, couldn't even vote. But he was a rascal, Takao, he ran up to Alaska looking for gold, had a story of how he ate his shoes, cave-ins, wolves, eggs for ten cents in the Yukon! But Dad was the older brother. They didn't get along. Too wild, he said, tsumaranai... but when Takao died, it broke his heart.... Kathy?"

Kathy shakes her head.

"You know, I just can't believe it Mum. I haven't seen you in three years and I come up here... You're telling a complete stranger things you've never told me. I mean, you've never made udon before, not that I've seen. And never a word of Japanese. I mean, I've been used to you ignoring me but this is really ridiculous. I come up here and we — I just..." She pushes herself away from the table, to the living room.

Norma Nakashima rises. "I thought you wanted me to get to know Gen."

"Mum," Kathy's head is still shaking, "You never talk. You've never given me any kind of... I didn't even know about Takao. I mean, with Robbie I can understand, but Gen, you don't even know her.

She's mine." Kathy grips herself. "She's my friend. You never talk about it. I mean the stuff about the war, about anything."

Norma Nakashima sits on the couch. From here she can see Belmont Park and a glimpse of the river. The sun slips low, burning red against the sky.

"I was ten years old when the evacuation began. They called it an 'evacuation' then. Our boat was seized. We never did get it back. We lost everything. And then Slocan. It was too unbelievable to be true. We were Canadians. Before we were evacuated there were so many rumours. Police searches, questionings, arrests. The papers screamed about fifth columnists. All those lies, all that hate. I didn't know people could hate so much. They arrested the Japanese language school teachers first, the shimbun people. Mr. Sato, when he was arrested, he put on his uniform from the First World War. Robert was sent to Angler while we were in Hasting Park. And Michiko, she was sent to Sandon and I never saw her again. Even after the war... It wasn't enough that we couldn't go back. Traitors, spies, they said. So many left. Take what you can carry, that's what they told us, what you can carry. Everything's safe. So many lies. Dispersal or deportation. What they called choices." She closes her eyes. "We'd been living on Powell Street. If you could have seen it before the war, you'd know. I remember waking up in the middle of the night. My window was blazing red. I looked outside and saw my father, my brothers and sisters in the yard by a giant fire. I ran downstairs. Mother was crying, laying things out. Outside they were all standing by the fire, burning everything, everything Japanese. Records, coats, pictures, shawls. All the books of my childhood, my mother's heirlooms, my dolls. My mother, she had tried so hard... We burned all of that, everything, to prove we were loyal, that we were Canadians. That night we took our English names. We became different people." Her voice falls to a whisper, eyes closed against the conflagration. "But you see, they imprisoned us just the same." She looks up. "Do you understand? We were nothing to them. Nothing." She stands, places her hands in her lap. "Good night Kathy," she whispers and walks into her room.

Kathy lies on the bed, staring at the ceiling. It is over. Over before she had even been born.

\ 45

Be quiet, be good. All the lessons on fitting in: good English, good education, a smile and a nod. Don't complain. The nail that sticks out gets hammered down.

Late nights, her mother and father at the kitchen table, in conversations too low for the children to hear. But heard just the same. Caught the fear. Don't be difficult, don't be different. Rocking boats flounder, sleeping dogs lie.

And what makes you think you could get away, run. History hunts you down, tracks of blood, tracks of bone.

The wooden floor creaks as Gen hovers like a ghost on the threshold. "Kathy. Are you all right?"

"God," Kathy folds, "I am useless."

"No, no." Gen stands close, circle of her arms. Kathy presses herself into softness, gazes at the scar beneath her chin. A familiar comfort, trace of hand, caressing thigh, an ache that hollows into soul.

Afterwards, Kathy is never sure that she hadn't dreamt it all.

Gen lies beside her, her body light with sleep, her arm thrown across Kathy's belly, her head by Kathy's shoulder. Kathy, her body heavy with pleasure, drifting from the surface of her dreams.

She feels the covers pull around her.

Kathy snaps awake.

In the dim light of the table side lamp she sees her mother slipping the blanket around her, across Gen, easily, as if she had done this a thousand times. This, turning her gaze into Kathy's eyes, she strokes back Kathy's hair and turns off the lamp, and just as easily leaves them to their rest.

Kathy lies back feeling bare, exposed, and, if ever she could have known it, bereft.

When Kathy wakes Gen is no longer beside her. She walks to the washroom. She dresses, folding up the bed, packing her things, quickly, quickly, with an edge of panic snapping at her heels.

She knocks at Gen's door.

"Gen?" Gen sprawls across the bed, her nightshirt thrown onto the floor. Her small Kannon, held between her breasts. As she gazes at her, Kathy wonders, why would she need mercy?

46 /

"Gen, time to get up." Gen opens her eyes, stretching, smiling. "We should go soon if we want to make it home by nightfall," Kathy adds.

By the time Gen is dressed, Norma Nakashima is in the kitchen making breakfast, as if it were in the usual scheme of things. "Good morning," she calls out as they emerge from Gen's room. "A good breakfast before you go. It'll ease the trip."

They sit down, chattering about the drive, the weather. Yet the knot in Kathy's stomach does not go away. They make their way to the car, throw in their bags and wait by the curb.

Norma Nakashima steps forward. "Gen, it was nice meeting you. I'm glad you know Kathy." She turns to Kathy, and gives her a soft hug, surprising them both. She steps back. "I'm glad for you both."

Kathy and Gen get in the car. Kathy turns, rolling down the window. She looks at her mother, greying hair and growing smaller. "Mum... take care of yourself."

Norma Nakashima smiles, waving to them as they pull out, down the drive. She sighs as they turn out of sight. Her mother's daughter. A grown woman after all, she thinks, and what could I give her. She clasps her hands and steps back into the apartment building.

There is lots to give,
She needs support, help,
a Mother.

\ 47

Mappings

Naomi takes a deep breath as the sky sparkles darkly, her belly tightens with a wheezing protest from her lungs. Her sighs seep into her shoulders as she kicks at the red and yellow leaves that drift from the branches. Dying, dying, dying. Why such a celebration when winter is just around the corner? She stomps at a piece of jack-o-lantern that has scattered her way. At least the annual slaughter of pumpkins is over.

Naomi glances at her watch, shrugs against the chill. She slumps her way into Future Bakery. The light of the foggy windows glows against her damp autumn mood, glancing off the copper-top tables, the wicker chairs. Students cluster by the coffee counter, and two others brood over a chess board. The rack of fresh bread is nearly empty but there is the smell of steaming coffee, borscht frothing in the tureen, buttery baked potatoes.

At the back, Sandy waves from her table. Nao slides into a chair by the window, facing Brunswick.

"How've you been?"

Naomi grunts.

Sandy rubs her hands together. "I guess that sums it up."

"I dunno. I just don't know."

"Listen, the last thing they need is for us to take sides in this. We can't give up on them just because they broke up."

"I'm not giving up on Gen. Or Kathy for that matter. I just don't get it."

"We can't do anything about it. They just have to..." Sandy's hand flails in the air, "work it through."

"Gen's the one getting burned."

Sandy frowns. "And how do you know that? Do you live with them? Do you have any idea what they are going through?"

"Fuck it man, I don't even know why people are together, let alone why they come apart. You'd figure something would work out. What the hell. In a few months we'll be bombing the shit out of a country most of us couldn't even find on a map. All because some American dickhead wants to walk softly and carry a big prick." Naomi sulks, ruffling her short hair with her fingers. "And I'm premenstrual with no girlfriend and two mid-terms coming up."

"See this?" Sandy leans forward, rubbing her thumb and forefinger together. "It's the world's smallest violin, and it's playing just for you." She stands. "Now, do you want some coffee?"

"It'll give me cramps," Naomi mutters sullenly, but as Sandy walks away she calls for a double expresso.

Sandy returns with the cups and saucers, steam rising above the dark liquid. Naomi peers into Sandy's cup.

"Peppermint tea? Sandy, have you gone granola on me? You're getting worse than those crystal heads."

Sandy only shrugs. "Some of us aren't as young as we used to be. Besides, I don't want to be the one bouncing off the walls at three in the morning."

"Hm." Naomi thoughtfully stirs her coffee. "What do you think'll happen?"

"Well, the Americans will bomb Iraq, Iraq will bomb Israel, Israel will bomb Iraq, Syria and Jordan will bomb Israel, then the Americans will start bombing everything. Then, out of the blue, over the rainbow, someone will bomb the Americans — and they'll miss and hit us."

Naomi scowls, "I was talking about Kathy and Gen."

Sandy takes a sip of her tea, purses her lips. "They need a little time to themselves. They need to keep away from each other. We have to keep out of it. Be supportive but not take sides. And try not to get into a rut about it, okay? I can just see you and Gen muttering until doomsday."

"What are you and Kathy going to see tonight?"

"The *East is Red* is playing at the Far East Theatre. Love, betrayal and tragic death."

"Great. Kathy's going to feel really great after seeing that."

"And what are you going to see?" Sandy sneers. "Some guy in a rubber suit, stepping on cardboard cars and tossing around paper mache."

"*Godzilla* is a metaphor, rising out of the atomic ashes, to wreak vengeance upon the world. Our fears in the nuclear age, the return of the repressed, the uncontrollable id!"

"Christ!"

"Well, at a time like this, we should be thinking about the end of the world."

Sandy sips her peppermint tea, wincing at the heat.

"Why does the world go crazy every couple of years, Sandy?"

"World is always crazy. We just don't hear about it half the time. An American-backed dictator can kill as many people as he wants to, as long as he tows the line. The minute he steps over it, he's demonized, and Bush's approval points go sky high." She shrugs, "Journalism's just press releases and photo ops. It's all Wall Street anyway. 'Collateral damage,' my ass."

"Thanks. You're just the one to cheer Kathy up."

Sandy puts down her cup. "If the sight of Lin Ching Hsia and Joey Wong tangled in the sheets doesn't cheer anyone up, then they're past death. Think of it: two cross-dressing dykes conquering the world."

Naomi smiles. "You and your world conquest stories."

"Well, it's good to plan ahead."

Sandy lies on the edge of sleep, snuggling under her fuzzy electric blanket. Tomorrow is the weekend, she reminds herself, she can sleep in, snooze through the entire day if she wants. She turns, trying to envision Lin Ching Hsia in suit and tie in *Peking Opera Blues*, Maggie Cheung in *Song of the Exile* and *Dragon Inn*. Sandy rolls to her side,

\ 51

shaking her head. Kathy had been restless during the entire film, distracted over coffee, her exhaustion etched clearly in her face. Grief, grief. Why does everyone assume the dumpee has the worst time of it?

The lamp flicks on in front of her eyes.

"Sandy?" Naomi hisses, her sax strap dangling in her pjs. "Sandy, are you asleep?"

She struggles through the sudden brightness. "Nao? What's wrong?" She blinks, clearing her eyes. But Naomi has already bounced beside her onto the bed, beneath the covers.

"It's cold. Did you call the landlord? The furnace hasn't kicked in and my room is fucking fureezing."

"You wanted the bay window."

Naomi groans loudly.

"Alright, alright, you can stay. But only if you're quiet. The neighbours'll think — "

"You've finally got lucky."

"You're one to talk." Sandy pulls the blanket to her side. "In my case it isn't luck. Strategy is everything."

"Maybe that's the problem. You're all analysis and no action."

"Sistah, the fish jus' ain't bitin'."

"If you ask me, you're fishing up the wrong creek."

"Yeah, and I ask you all the time, don't I?" Vexed, she turns her back. But she has to admit that Naomi is right. Veronica, the leitmotif in the opera of her life. Screwed up straight chicks who fall in love with lesbians. Is there a song for that? Christ, there is no way of getting around it; she is truly and deeply fucked.

"Now, you hafta know what you want or else you end up getting screwed, chewed and barbecued," Naomi is saying.

"What?"

Naomi props herself up with her elbow. "You haven't been listening to me, have you?"

"Not if it's a lecture, Nao."

"Ya gotta know what you want to get it. Now a lotta dykes looking for sex end up getting married because of the damn couplism of the community. It's hard just to fuck around."

"Aw, poor baby."

Naomi sits up. "Tell me, what does a lesbian bring to her first date? Her furniture. And what do they eat the morning after? Even their cereal is monogamous."

"Hey, in this age of safer sex —"

"What about it? Do you think monogamy's gonna protect you from AIDS? A nice little cocoon, a harbour from the storm? What about all that stuff that comes with safer sex, all that stuff that gets lumped in with the fucking? How it becomes twisted into this one person who'll satisfy all your needs and desires. Eternity and forever and happily ever after. And all the damn pressure from 'the community.'"

"Nao —"

"It's pretty damn het if you ask me. Like the song says, 'you're nobody, til somebody loves you.'"

"I'll never get to sleep."

"No, really. It's always, 'Hey Nao, seeing anyone yet?' Or they're trying to set me up with someone they know. Or they see me with a woman, and boom, we gotta be lovers, I mean, we're dykes, aren't we?"

"It was that damned coffee, wasn't it?"

"Or your close friends. You see them every day when they're single. When they get a lover, they fall into 'The Void,'" Naomi's voice booms ominously. "Don't see them, don't hear from them, just one long beep on the answering machine."

"Alright, alright. Now sleep."

With the lights off, they settle in.

"Sandy?" Naomi's muffled voice rises from the blanket.

"Yes."

"If you got a lover, would you kick me out?"

"In a second, kiddo. Now go to sleep."

"Sandy?"

Sandy rolls over, pillow over head.

"Sandy, I can't sleep."

The only sound is the thwump of an incoming pillow at ninety miles an hour.

Early evening and Joan Armatrading sings of love and persuasion. In front of her bathroom mirror, Naomi Chiba draws herself to her full four feet and ten inches. She ties back her bandanna, tugs at her vest, biting fretfully on her lip. I'll never make it to butch, she curses, knowing that to some eyes she'd barely make baby dyke, let alone baby butch. As an Asian dyke she is invisible, not big enough for butch, not white enough for femme, invisible among the exoticized, eroticized shadows of street lights and bars. But it's more than that. Nao pulls at her ears. Too cute for words, Sharmini had teased. Cute. As in kittens or bugs in rugs. But Gen could pull it off. She had always had that edge of... something: the strong, silent type. Maybe that had been the problem, Naomi reflects. Screwed, chewed. She rocks on her heels, deflated.

Naomi is meeting Sharm and Ana at the bar. Maybe tonight she won't be asked for I.D. Maybe tonight they'll play some salsa or bhangra and not the usual techno/industrial hell. And then again, maybe George Bush will turn the defence budget over to the homeless, Mulroney's jaw will lock and the Martians will finally phone home.

She looks down at her feet. Sami had already called to say she couldn't, wouldn't make it. She'd been meeting with her partner for days. *Processing*, Nao mutters. Like cheese. Does not sound healthy. And Sandy and Veronica — Naomi could only throw her hands up — she'd throw up more if she could. Karma, auras, magnetic fields, catastrophes all. But not for her. No, thank god. Nao figures that there is only one thing in this world you can count on and that is your saxophone. Your saxophone is always there, answers when you call, cries when you cry — never ignores you, or talks down to you, or stays out late on Saturday night, except with you, of course. Never too tired, or too broke, or too something.

Naomi steps back from the mirror.

Then there is Clara. Drop dead gorgeous and single to boot. Enough to make anyone's ovaries spin. Clara at the refugee forum, smiling as she handed out the pamphlets. She gave a great presentation but Naomi had been too busy staring to take notice. She'd be at the bar tonight, or so Ana promised. Not that it really matters, Naomi reminds herself. It isn't what she's looking for. No, not another soul-destroying, time-consuming addiction, a second-rate melodrama of fusion and delusion. It's a favour to Ana. Another companera, freezing in these Canadian winters, she'd said. So they'd meet at the bar at eleven — Ana, Sharmini, Clara and Naomi.

Nao, not a fool, could smell the set up a mile away. But still... Saturday night... and Clara.

The bar flashes neon. Bass and rhythm rippling through air, murmurings, like a rush beneath the skin. In the cool November air you can see the misty hellos of women hanging out by the entrance of the bar, cloudy imprints of laughter against darkness. Naomi steps inside, slaps down the two dollar cover and begins pushing her way through the crowd of women, side-stepping elbows, trays, and cigarette butts. In an alcove by the stairs she shrugs off her leather jacket, throwing off the outside chill, as her eyes scan the dance floor. She leans against the banister. Bars have never been entirely comfortable for her — white bread boxes of trendoid clones and existential cool. Too much attitude and desperate need: the fatal combination of cruising an' boozing. But dyke bars always held fascination, the preppy Rose, or Dyke Nites at the cool cold Boom, the clash of leather and grunge. The Warehouse, Felines, and Cariboo had all closed, as well as Chez Moi. Dyke dances are few and far between. There is Lola's, strobes and white smoke against a cavernous interior.

Behind her, two women shout over the music:

"Oh come on, she's gotta be — "

"Linda, you read everyone as a dyke, or dyke potential. Get a grip."

"Well, I'm just saying her D.P. has a very high rating."

"Christ, it's like you sitting around listening to that Tracy Chapman song for four hours, trying to track down her personal pronouns."

"I'm telling you Melissa Etheridge is a dyke, just listen to her songs, I mean who else would say 'romeo —'"

Christ, the crowd is getting younger by the minute, Naomi thinks as she sees a group of grunge dykes by the bar. She glances down to the jukebox, the pool table, a room of faces, dim lights and cigarettes. The brick wall and faces. The stairway and patio and faces. She laughs, air filling lungs deep into her belly.

Clara stands by the doorway, her torn denim jacket on her arm, her hand rustling through her dark cropped hair. Absently, she tugs at her red armband. As she squints against darkness and smoke, she takes in the length of the bar, her eyes resting for a moment on the trio in the corner as they throw back their shooters. Clara looks away. She shrugs, feels the stitch in her shoulder. Why are they meeting here, she mutters? The smoke catches at her throat and she has a sudden urge for a scotch.

"Hola," Naomi steps out from behind her with a smile, her voice raised above the blasting music. "Como estas? Have you seen Ana and Shar?"

Clara shakes her head and turns, almost shouting. "They will be late, as always." Her eyes flick to the tv above the bar. An elbow jabs in her back.

"How's it been going?" Naomi asks.

How to explain that the grant did not come through, that Maria's hearing is in two days, that her bus was late twenty minutes and an old man threw up on her shoes?

"Fine," says Clara.

The crowd pushes them forward.

"Hot," Nao pulls at her shirt. "It's like an oven in here."

"I've sworn never to complain about heat," Clara runs her hand through her hair. "It's the cold that kills you."

"Ana told me you hated the winters. How long have you been in Canada?"

"Five years. Very long years." Here, in el culo del diablo, Clara silently curses. She glances down at Naomi, at her short hair and soft cherubic face, and mutters, "Ana and her crazy ideas. I should be in bed." Clara stretches her shoulders, her back, "I should be home."

"What?" Nao leans forwards.

Clara shakes her head.

"What do you think about the music?"

Clara shrugs noncommittally. The smoke is beginning to sting her eyes.

"Do you want to dance?"

Clara shifts uncomfortably. "I'm not a very good dancer."

"I wouldn't have thought it. Ana says — "

"Why?" Clara's voice hardens, "Do you think I'm one of those hot latina dykes? Wild chicas?"

Naomi flounders, "No, I just... I mean..."

Clara turns away.

Naomi looks down at her feet. She's blown it. Glancing up, she murmurs an exit, "Gotta go to the can."

Clara watches Naomi thread her way through the crowd. She shakes her head. "Well, Ana should have known better than to set me up with a baby dyke," she growls, "Jail bait if ever I saw it."

But it is more than that. Clara suddenly feels drained. She feels the push of bodies, the dust on her lungs, the life leeching out of her pores. She stumbles to the patio, a gasp as the heat falls away. She rubs her eyes, feels the grit against her eyeball, her tears against her hand. She looks up. "*La noche esta estrellada, y tiritan, azules, los astros, a lo lejos,*" Clara whispers. She sits and listens to the screech of the streetcar, down on the curve of Carlton.

From the safety of the patio, Clara gazes into the windows of the bar, the dance floor, the pool table, the jukebox. She can see the different groups of women, and Naomi, weaving through larger, oblivious bodies, the push, pull of the crowd. Clara closes her eyes. She sighs, her gaze floating across the sky.

But Clara waits. And feels Nao beside her with her jacket in hand.

"Are you leaving?" Clara asks, then shakes her head, "Of course.... Just out of curiousity, how old are you?"

"Twenty-four," Naomi replies.

Clara purses her lips. Hesitates. "You speak Spanish."

"Enough to get by. But I've lost a lot of it. I don't use it very often, so it... floats away."

"Yes."

"When you lose a word, it's like a part of you disappears."

"And your Japanese?"

Naomi shrugs, palms open.

Clara nods. "You know, I have been in this country for five years. And I am so tired. Tired of explaining my life to these First World babies, tired of the winters, the language, tired of the bar scene and tired of the games. I wonder, is it too much to ask to go home, to the mountains." To the market, the candles burning at Chichicastenangos, the lights at Tayasal.

Clara leans against the pillar and feels a tightness slip from her shoulders. She begins to speak again, but stops, gazes at the pattern of light and smoke in the air. Strangely enough, it is Clara who reaches out, brushing back Naomi's hair, looking into her eyes, hands stroking behind her ears, curling into the fine lines of her neck. Releasing her, she feels the slightest tremble, the body sending a message of its own, without translation.

Nao's fingers slip down Clara's arm, down the length of muscle, past the wrist, fingers stroking open, the palm of her hand. "Manos." She lifts Clara's hand to her lips, tongue tracing lines, and with a final kiss, she leaves them.

Her hands reach up to Clara's face, the dark shadows of her eyes. Naomi steps closer, encircled by her, Clara's arms closing around her waist, her hips pressing deeper. Was it always like this, this heaviness and desire, this reckless greed? "I always get it mixed up... cejas, senos?"

Hold. She takes a breath. Knees shake, step away. A confusion, where touch begins, the skin of her, and her.

And hips, the rocking playfulness of hips, the dip of thigh, the pressing tension as she tries to hold her to this, as her tongue rolls around and into the curve of her ears, this roar of senses, of mouth chasing lips, even as the sharpness of her fingers pinches her nipples, teasing, rising with the pull of her cunt.

But Clara, her fingers, feels the hollow and gasp, strokes through the roughness of Nao's jeans. She discovers pockets and slips into them, inside, and she's there.

Beneath the evening sky, Clara stands, pressed against Nao, rocking, her hips moving against her, her tongue in the curl of ear, as she strokes with such strength and such care, holding her in her hands with the hope that such promises could be forever.

"Well, I see you two have found each other," Sharm's voice cuts in, reprovingly.

Naomi nearly collapses against Clara as she straightens. She shakes her head, she tries to focus above the spinning lights, the music. But she can see Sharm's crooked smile working its way around her lips and Ana's averted blush. And God, she can still feel the heated imprint of Clara's hand and the tell-tale weakness of her knees.

"Ah, yes." Naomi cringes at her own voice; it was like getting caught with your fingers in the cookie jar.

"I guess you two don't need an introduction." Sharm doesn't even try to hide her smirk. "Looks like a pretty in-depth discussion to me."

Naomi closes her eyes, repeats to herself that people can not actually die of embarrassment.

Clara replies in an even tone, "Yes, it was a very interesting talk." She turns to Naomi. "I'd like to continue it, maybe over coffee?" She gestures towards the door.

Naomi nods, not trusting her voice.

"I'll see you then, manana," Clara waves to Sharm and Ana, ⌣ scuttles out the door.

Outside they burst out laughing, echoes rolling down the deserted street. With the crispness of the air, pools of light falling from above, their laughter falters. Her breathing sharp, the sudden stillness — hush. It is late, late. Nao turns to Clara. "I live down the street. It's not too far... and we could get out of the cold."

Clara takes her hand, smiles. "My house is just around the corner."

Naomi smiles back and thinks, hey, who needs to be butch.

Naomi traces the constellation of scars along Clara's back. In sleep Clara seems at peace, caught in the rhythm of her dreams. A soft murmur and she turns, as open as she would never be in the waking light. Naomi reflects on the contrast of Clara in sleep. In sleep do we shed the world, returning to ourselves? Naomi can only wonder. Cautiously she shifts, settles into the blanket. Her gaze follows the foot of the bed, to the collage of images on Clara's desk. To newspaper clippings and photographs. To the walls covered in maps, like arteries, like veins. Transit maps, tourist maps, streets scrawled on napkins, cities etched by scribes, antique maps, shredded maps, maps of imaginary cities, mythical and historical, maps of probability, of possibility. Maps of nerve ends, circulatory and skeletal systems. Palm maps, facial maps. A cartography of the retina, a topography of the heart. Maps of the homes to the stars.

Nao slips out of the bed, her hand on the face of a city. Her finger traces. Wellesley to Harbord to Novae Insvlae to corpus callosum.

The wall brightens, the head of the lamp twisted, naked bulb. Naomi turns.

"Wh.... oh Naomi..." Clara, propped on her elbow.

Naomi sees the calm settle into Clara's eyes. "I'm sorry. I woke you." She slides under the sheets, shivers. "You should sleep."

"No," Clara yawns, "Once I open my eyes... I am awake."

Nao studies her. "Do you have a fear of getting lost?"

"What? Oh, the maps. No, not a fear of getting lost. You're shivering." She pulls the blanket around Nao, lies back. A map of Central America pinned to the ceiling. She smiles. "It must seem strange."

"I'm just curious. I have a few snow globes, so I can relate."

"Snow globes?"

"Yeah. You know, glass balls. With snow in them."

"You keep balls of snow..."

"They're glass."

"Ah." Clara shakes her head. "Snow in glass. The people in this country are crazy."

"Yeah, they have houses in them, and when you turn them over... never mind."

"Do they have stars, these globes?"

"I suppose so."

"Look." Clara clicks off the lamp. Stars sprinkle her ceiling, her walls. She whispers "*La noche esta estrellada, y tiritan, azules, los astros, a lo lejos*, do you know their light takes millions of years to reach us, they are so far. Do you think they knew, that their journey would take them such an impossible distance, such an impossible faith? How does it go... *Pero... pero es bello amar al mundo con los ojos.... los ojos...* Ah, it is gone."

Clara stretches, turning, her body arches open.

Naomi looks away.

Clara catches her glance. "Ah, you are a shy one," and strokes the gentle slope of belly against a sharpness of breath. She slips down, taste of salt, pulling.

Clara gazes down on Naomi's face, the scent of her imprinted on flesh. Nao lies curled, eyes closed. Their hands are clasped, fingers entwined. Such small hands. Clara strokes the thick blackness of Naomi's hair, shivers at such frailty. She closes her eyes. A body turning in sleep can betray so much. Yet her eyes still trace the light of stars thrown long ago, against this living, breathing flesh. She gazes down at Naomi. In sleep we seem so alone. And when we wake? With the eyes of those yet to be born.

night
crossing

Gen Tanaka shrugs her way into the sleeves of her long woollen coat, laces her scuffed leather boots and sets out to where her father is dying. Above her the first snowflakes hover, encumbered by the light evening breeze. Gen stretches out her hand — then fist — as the crystalline prisms fizzle against her skin. Transmutation, Gen thinks, ice, to water, to air. The sky is close and cloudy, a puffy glowing grey. As she runs across Queen Street for the streetcar, a car horn blasts, followed by a sharp obscenity and a skyward finger. Gen turns. A scathing retort churns in her stomach, rises to her throat, but vanishes in the misty air. Hollow. She catches a snowflake on her tongue. A screech of tracks as the red streetcar doors open in front of her. She squeezes her way through bundles and packages, reflects upon the malevolence of the universe, then a seat opens to her left, single, by the window. She brushes the fog from the glass and taps her boots together. The snow falls faster, heavier. At University she trudges off the streetcar. On the corner, a red cart man rubs his hands over the open oven of roasted chestnuts, peanut bags, popcorn. Gen walks down to the subway, into the shuttling metal sausages and squeezes off at Queen's Park. In the labyrinth of tunnels, strip malls of the underworld, she loses her bearings and stares at the redbluegreen map under fluorescence and neon.

"Do you need any help, sonny?" asks an older white man, with a long beard, red suit.

"Uh. Yeah. I'm looking for Bell Hospital."

"You're in it."

Gen looks around her, sees Tim Hortons. "Here?"

"Yeah, it's the food court. Upstairs, the hospital." His thumb points upwards.

"Thanks," Gen nods. She tugs at her small figure of Kannon that dangles around her neck and walks briskly to the elevator.

On the fifth floor of Thomas Bell Hospital, in critical care, Gen sits on the couch and places her cards for a game of solitaire. She has been in to see her father, a father she has not seen in close to ten years. She saw his tubes, his chart, his gaunt face and felt nothing. Nothing. In the washroom mirror she splashed her eyes, traced the scar, fluorescent light blinking overhead. She rubbed her forehead, wiped her mouth with a rough paper towel. In the waiting room she gazes out the window, to the falling snow. By the borders of the glass, festive lights flash red, green, blue, redgreenblue. She can hear the tinny music from the nurses' station down the hall. She shudders. A draft from the window. Nothing, she thinks. She owes him nothing.

And waits, shuffling spades, diamonds, hearts.

Gen's head jerks back, her eyes squint in dim light. She had dozed fitfully but the sky is still dark, filled with tiny perfect crystalline patterns. Her cards had scattered to the floor and she bends over, shoving them into an awkward pile. Knights, queens, jokers.

When Gen sits back she notices her, a shadow in the corner. Startled, Gen drops the cards again, stoops to retrieve them. A hello is lost in her throat, a gasp that she swallows.

The shadow steps out of the corner.

She is a little taller than Gen, with black, cropped, bristling hair. Like Gen, she wears glasses, although they sit perilously on the bridge of her nose, a frailty of wire and glass. Her face is broad, with a certain squareness of features, her head round, a maru daruma. Her hands are small, fingers curl, as if they hold delicate, wondrous creatures.

She clears her throat. "I'm Setsuko Nozoe," her voice low, almost a whisper.

"Gen Tanaka."

They exchange hesitant nods and sit down.

"I'm sorry I woke you."

"No." Gen shakes her head. "I was... waiting."

Setsuko folds her hands, eyes almost closed behind glass lenses. "My brother just came up from emergency."

Gen nods. She can hear the pat, pat, pat of nurses down the hall, beeps and buzzes of the station. And the wind, rising. Her gaze travels to the lights, the window, frantic waves of falling snow.

"Tanaka," Setsuko speaks suddenly, "as in the Tanakas of Toronto Nihongo Gako?"

"No. Tanaka as in room 505, Thomas Bell." Gen smiles. "Shin ijushya, you know."

"Ah."

"And you?"

Setsuko nods.

"Thought so. I kind of guessed by your name." Gen shuffles her cards, tap, tap against the formica table. "Have you seen your brother yet?"

"Once. I've been waiting downstairs, I don't know how long."

"Yes." Gen turns, as if she heard the drip of intravenous, a faint scratch of breath. "Everything seems to run at a snail's pace."

Setsuko gazes out the foggy window, draws a spiral against glass. She stares at her fingertip, the pattern of lines and whorls. "Snails are hermaphrodites, you know. They're born with shells, that's why geneticists use them, for the tracings on their shells. Mendel, he used snow peas but switched to hawkweeds — they're parthenogenetic. But Mendel didn't know. I mean about the nature of hawkweeds."

Click, flick, shuffle.

"Are you a biologist?"

"No," Setsuko shakes her head, "I'm an archivist. I study the dead

\ 63

bones of history." She looks at Gen, at the pin on her chest. "Ah," Setsuko smiles. "Tomboy."

Gen laughs, "I think I prefer dyke, myself."

"You wear the black triangle, not the pink."

Gen glances down at the pin. She had forgotten it altogether. "Lesbians were usually put in the camps with a black triangle, under the category of 'asocials.' Pinks were usually reserved for men."

She stretches and pushes away her cards. "If we're going to be here for the rest of the night, we might as well get comfortable. Can I get you some coffee, or some soup, or something? Vending machines are down the hall but there's a Tim Horton's in the underground mall thing."

Setsuko looks up, pushes back her glasses, a glint of light against the wire. "Sure. I'll come with you."

After following the yellow line to the blue line to the elevator, they stumble back to critical care. Setsuko stirs her cup of congealed clam chowder as Gen gingerly swallows bitter, over-boiled coffee. Her first sip burned both her tongue and the roof of her mouth. Even her teeth ache. Unlucky, Gen knows Nao will say, unlucky. She cuts the cards and shuffles with a flourish. As she turns to Setsuko, she slaps the deck between them.

"Here, pull a card and say the first thing that comes to mind."

"Truth or dare?"

"Whatever."

"How long?"

"Whatever. But it has to make sense, make some kind of a story."

Setsuko takes off her glasses, rubs her eyes. She draws her card. Red. Queen of hearts.

"My big, little brother, Akira is in hospital bed 524. He's the closest family I've got. I don't look anything like him, really. His hair is straight, long. He has my mother's hair. I don't live here, visiting, you know. I live in Calgary. Joanne, she's with her folks in Halifax and Kaori, she's in Van, so we thought it'd be good for me to come back, hang around for a while. Akira's in a band called BooBooKitty and they do a Shonen Knife kind of thing. After his gig at Lee's, he's beat up, gay-bashed on Sherbourne, helping Jimmy Sherman load the equipment, the drums an' stuff into his apartment. Akira's with Joanne.

They have a three year old, Aly, he calls her. Aly-Oops. He's good father. I don't know where he gets it from. Funny thing is my parents haven't seen Akira since he started seeing Joanne, around five years ago. They haven't even seen Aly-oop. They just can't stand the thought of Joanne being with Akira. You see, she's Black. Been in this country before damn Confederation, five generations in Nova Scotia. But in my parents' eyes... Suddenly, I'm the good kid in the family, queer as I am. Not the 'black sheep' anymore. The world is fucked. End of story."

Setsuko sighs. She picks up the card. Heart, queen of hearts. "Do you know," her voice whispers, "whales have hearts as big as cars..."

Gen picks up the deck, traces the pattern of swirls, white and blue. The whirl of shuffling cards, snow against glass, the electronic blink blink of lights, redbluegreen redbluegreen. She draws a nine of clubs.

"Once upon a time, I got caught playing with my father's katana. He'd left it on his chair in his room and I was never allowed in his room, but I snuck in whenever I got the chance. My dad collected katana. All of his stories of the forty-seven ronin, I figure, he must be like the last warrior — he had the whole bushido trip. I mean, we left Japan when I was so young, but I think he left because it was changing so much. I think he left to keep it the same in his mind. And that day that I ran into his room and touched his precious katana, he was so mad — but not just mad — he was mad with a purpose. He took me into my room and said that in one hour he was going to come and beat me. Then he just turned and sat down at his desk with his papers. And I waited. I heard everything. The drip of the faucet, the creak of his chair, even his papers rubbing together. It took so long but he kept his word. And even before he raised his hand, do you know what he told me? He said, I'm going to hit you ten times. If you cry you'll be slapped with ten more. I was nine years old."

Setsuko pulls her card and places it squarely in front of her. Diamonds. Four of diamonds.

"We used to live beside this hydro field, with big steel towers and grass, long, long grass, as far as you could see, and the wires that were strung between towers, following those lines, with everything getting high. You could just fall down in it and nobody'd find you it was so tall. In September, just after school started, the city crew would come an' cut the grass. It'd be like straw, what we thought was straw anyway, all dry and scratchy. We'd even smoke some of the stuff. Made straw forts an' burn 'em down. We'd play scarecrow. We'd try an' catch each other, stuff the hay down shirts an' pants, in our underwear. Weird, you know, that want-to-be-caught-but-don't-wanna-be thing. That excitement. One time, we were playing hide an' seek, and I was running into the field and it was the long, long grass. I ran and ran and then — I just stopped and fell backwards, like somebody'd catch me. The grass was so soft and green, green, that colour. Walls of green. I remember looking up at the hydro tower. It looked as if it was falling down but taking forever and I was just staring at it, waiting for the tower to fall, like in slow motion. Not afraid but waiting. It never fell. See?" Setsuko holds up her hands, her fingers in a triangle, "Diamonds, they look like diamonds."

Gen pulls a two of spades.

"I met Kathy at Take Back the Night, the time it was at Grange Park, near Dundas. There were crowds, a lot of people, mostly white folk, and I was setting up for the taiko drummers on stage. I think she'd just come from one of her collective meetings, and she looked wiped, just wiped. And I was checking out the crowd. Take Back the Night has a weird energy, always something happens, cops harassing, guys on the street. Doesn't have the feel of IWD or Pride Day, you know? It has an edge. Like it's dangerous.

"Anyway. Have you ever noticed, sometimes when you're in a bar and you see another Asian woman or a woman of colour and you just can't seem to catch her eye. Kind of sinks the notion of safety in numbers, solidarity forever, that kind of stuff. I don't know. Maybe it's like wallpaper, there but you don't see it. Or it's like passing. How does that work, do you think? I didn't talk to her that night. But I met her, later.

"And then it was different, all over again. Everything familiar and strange, at the same time. Like how your body just buzzes when she's in another part of the room, how you know, you just know that she's there, the way she just seeps into you, through the skin, on the tongue...

"We'd fight over the strangest things, you know. How she'd put shoyu on her rice, or she'd make sushi too big. Once, I'd teased her about being so tall, I said three generations of anglo food and boom, the sansei had sprouted like beans. She got so mad. Like I was calling her some kind of fake, some kind of failure.

"We broke up two months ago. I still haven't unpacked the boxes."

They trace the lines, green to blue, through the labyrinth of corridors. Like thieves, like children, they slip into room 524, into a contraction of space with the hiss of respirator, blue tinge of light falling onto waving curtains, the stern line of sheets. His eyes, sunken, the cup of breath, the sigh of the machines. Gen looks across to Setsuko: family resemblance, shape of nose, set of eyes, the small fine hands of fragile flesh and bone.

"Daruma-san koronda," Gen whispers.

Setsuko turns.

"A game we used to play," Gen explains, "once upon a time."

Setsuko strokes a lock of his thick black hair. "Last Christmas, I didn't have any time to spend with him. Christ, he hasn't even met Aiko or Masao."

"Who are...."

"Kaori's kids." Setsuko takes his cold hand, leans forward. "My kids." She shakes her head. "My god, Akira, Aly-Oops has cousins."

The wind, a flurry against the window. A passing cloud, and the moon shines, huge and white, into the rooms.

Gen takes off the cord that she always carries around her neck, the small figure of Kannon, and presses it into Akira's hand. She glances up at Setsuko. "Luck, the goddess of mercy."

Setsuko pauses. "Your father...."

But Gen is out the door, down the blue hallway, the maze of lines.

Setsuko lies on the couch, her eyes, open, close, touch and go. The lights still blink redgreenblue, redgreenblue, as the clock measures out the seconds as Gen sits, placing, replacing her cards.

"Kaori has a hectic, hectic life. I think she even dreams in fast motion. She's very precise. Direct. But me, I'm kind of fuzzy. I take the long way around things. But having kids, they change everything, everything gets bundled together. Like going to the dentist, buying everything gets bundled together. Like going to the dentist, buying groceries, picking them up after school and daycare, dinnertime, bathtime, bedtime, everything running together. And the house is a mess, and you've forgotten tomorrow is hot dog day, or they pee the bed, or nightmares, so they curl up with you and they sleep, or they cry... like angels. You hope for the best.

"Last September, when we were up on Nose Hill and I had this kite, shaped like a hawk. Big wings. I was sitting down, Aiko beside me. The sky was blue, blue for miles and you could see the mountains in the west, really clearly, like teeth biting into the sky. Nose hill looks over the city, with that wind, and the kite flying high. Aiko's so small. She's three years old. She was holding the string, that plastic roll thing, and she kept on letting it go. And I'd run, run to the rescue, jump over gopher holes, grass and thistles, get the damn string, bring it back, tie it up on the roll and I'd give it back to her. I did it three damn times before I figured out that she wanted to see it fly, really fly. She wasn't afraid of losing it, or letting it go. And me, chasing that damned piece of string."

Gen turns, hears the wheeze of the respirator down the hall. Setsuko's eyes flutter. She sighs, eyes closed. "Bats can hear in the dark. They cry out and echoes bounce off, like in a cavern or a mountain. They have wings but it's only skin that folds up when they sleep. And they dream together, hanging from the mouths of caves and when they cry, it's like rain. Sloths are so slow that moss grows on them and turns them green. They smile and they're upside down. Does that mean they frown?"

"I don't know. I don't know."

Setsuko sleeps as the light creeps into dawn, as Gen flips the cards and shuffles, flips and shuffles. Outside, the sharp, glittering snow, the empty space of wind, of morning.

68 /

Bird
Box
Lantern

light, white, reflects against snow. cold, the crispness of air, dry, crunch, as ice snaps beneath heel.

gen holds her arm up against the sun.

my father is dying, dying, she repeats silently. and remembering in the flooding bleakness of the day: my father is dead.

walking aimlessly, her legs take her to the park, skeleton of trees, stillness against a pale blue light and below, a river.

the bird. the bird. it seems a miracle. dark wings across a bitter sky. a drop of red, rises, darts from sight.

gen motionless. call it. birds are always messengers. call it, turn and walk away.

she feels the prayer beads slip from her fingers. call it. there are no miracles. as she closes her eyes, she feels a moment's vertigo, swaying, as if brushed by wings.

gen walks to the house on Bathurst. corner, fence, peeling white paint, a small backyard, verandah slap against pavement. she takes her shoes off by the doorway, the smell of temple incense greets her in the hall.

her father's house.

with her hand along the hallway, she feels the notches on the door: gen at four, at seven, time cut into deadwood, scars marking passage. the floorboards creak by the stair, in the forbidden room, the desk, her father's collection of katana, thin sheet thrown across single bed, a bureau gathering a film of dust. fifty-two years for this.

on his desk, a pen, pages against the spare oak, a wooden box, string, a mountie pocket knife. floral wallpaper, velvet red. glass marbles in a bottle, light refracting through seven coloured spheres. a paper lantern, crushed. in the chest by the bedroom, an armful of letters, musty, with the grain of fallen leaves.

excavating, gen thinks. the only word that comes to mind.

cuff links, tie pin, the familiar scrawl of her father's hand. a notebook, pages fallen open to a photograph.

gen: the camera always lies.

light catches surface, air and space a fluid, frozen and preserved, as if a moment could be held, like a bottle, or a knife. photograph: gen at two years, asleep in a train seat. the landscape is blurred, cliffs in the distance. it must be near izu, between the mountains and the sea. reflected in the window, behind the photograph, behind the eye of the camera, outside of the frame: gen's mother.

close your eyes. trace of incense.

what she remembers are the lullabies, the songs bridging sleep and dreams, the storytimes spoken in a mothertongue broken, broken of her simple love of words. her refusal to speak to him, his language.

gen sets down the photograph.

her mother. her father. the only thing she knew, the only way of being, of being Japanese. what was there, after all? empty room, a photograph, threads all unravelling.

they leave, they always leave you.

in the bathroom, head under the tap.

mirror, mirror.

she sifts through letters, the neat script of her grandmother's hand. as she pushes herself from desk and papers, she catches sight of the beaten trunk, waiting, in the corner of the room.

it had been hers, many years ago, an old blue metal trunk, scored and

dented. but hadn't she buried it years ago? gently she opens its clasps, easing the heavy lid back on hinges.

inside, pages and pages. a child's drawing of a fiery sun. urutoraman and godzilla, orange and red, plastic toys from botan candy, wrappers from gilco. a child's handprint, a card cut from foolscap. a package of nori, faded brown. gen smiles, remembers the game: i can eat black paper.

she closes the lid and steps into the kitchen.

on the wall, a photograph: gen at seven, on her father's shoulders, capturing a moment's truce between them. as she closes her eyes she can imagine a running wind close against her body, a sky clear and low, the pebbled sound of river as a bullrush unravels in her hands. dragonflys, bright, shards of perfection.

lies.

he got out of it. all blame. my father is dead.

why, why did she marry him?

she steps into the room, gathers the paper lantern, plastic toys. in the backyard she collects them all, places them in the long forgotten trunk. she goes back for the photograph, taken from her father's kitchen. with a swift stroke she breaks the glass and throws it onto the pile. matchsticks scatter, a fumble with the box. as she stands back, she burns the relics of her childhood. burns the broken chair, the lantern, crayon, books, all in the beaten trunk. flames licking the photograph, curling image into darkness, pages fluttering, as if with wings.

karasu.

Rabbit Moon

It has been fifteen hours, travelling with the sun. Gen chews her lip, her ears popping in the descent. The plane rattles to a halt, she resets her watch. Time zones clashing in the geography of the heart. The other side of the world.

As she disembarks, she thinks of destinations and arrivals, airports as points of transition in the mapping of lives: claustrophobia of rubber seats and recycled air, the terse in-between state of corridors. Disorientation, she thinks, bodies flux, in motion. She follows the crowd in a blind fatigue, endless lines of customs, baggage, to the bursting release of the great glass doors.

Faces, faces. Japanese faces. Homecoming.

She steps across the barrier, trying to push through the bottleneck in the crowd. "Suimasen, suimasen," her head nods with every step. She pulls her luggage clear — and freezes. Before her stands a small white-haired woman, stooped, smiling.

Startled, "Bachan —" Gen begins. Grandmother.

"Gen-chan," the old woman greets her. "Sa ne, kaerimasho."

Gen is restless on the bus, still unbelieving. The green calm of Chiba is slowly replaced by the endless sprawl of Tokyo. At Tokyo Eki, her grandmother punches in at the automated ticket machine, Gen stands, dazed. The signs: Ueno, Yamanote, Marunouchi. Shinkansen, and Bachan waves the green tickets for platform thirteen, the Kodama.

On the platform they choose their car and set down their bags as marker. Gen wipes the sweat off her face with a handkerchief that Bachan has given her: Hello Kitty and Anpanman. Absently, she plays with the yen in her pocket and eyes the ubiquitous vending machines. Further down are small booths, selling magazines, books, and bento boxes. Gen checks her luggage — the all-important o-miyage bag is still there. Lose your passport, lose your money, but don't lost your presents. Gen laughs. Perhaps she is not quite the gaijin that she makes herself out to be. Voices catch at her, snatches of belonging, restless murmurings of her heart. Was it a trick of memory, a sleight of longing — that time has not passed, that all is the same and nothing lost. Kawa, mizu, mizumi. She searches her mind for words. Mothertongue come back to me, she whispers, and yet here I am, her eyes bright and hungry. To her left a woman and her young daughter stand, hand in hand. Farther down, past the businessmen, students queue in their separate clusters. They wear the same strict uniforms that Gen had seen thirteen years ago. Familiar, yet estranged. Bachan seems the same, greyer, smaller. Gen catches herself. Suddenly she has a family — but of course — Bachan had been a distant reality in Canada. Yet, flesh and blood, here she is, greeting Gen as if she had seen her only yesterday. Grandmother. I'm not an orphan anymore, Gen realizes. For in the land of your ancestors, how can you be alone?

Through the window of the train, Gen sees the mountains, always mountains, the flat river and miles and miles of green. Rice fields, emerald and jade, flooded paddies mirroring the sky. Carved out of hills and mountain sides, the sculpted tea bushes round the steepness of the land, calming waves. Bamboo thickets, sloping tiles of roofs, stone forests of family shrines.

Gen gazes out, enraptured. Home. Home, of longing, of joy. Atami, where her grandfather had lived. The river where Gen fished long ago.

Bachan grasps her arm. They were nearing Shizuoka. "Gen-chan, mieru?"

74 /

Gen peers at the sky. Tracing through clouds, Fujisan, magic mountain. "Hai, mieru."

The landscape unscrolls before her eyes and she sees it — Daishowa — the letters bold across the factory wall. The world spins in cold, astronomical space. Gen reflects, you always think of the enemy as the other, but how are you implicated in these stories of homeland and return? The sign out the window, flashing by, flash of an eye.

But she remembers. A retina memory.

Gen lies on the futon, her body held still, as if to feel the gravitational spin of earth and sky, pull of centre, in the room in which she had been born. Shoji, the symmetry of line, of moonlight falling against spare tatami.

Looking through the miles of the day it seems impossible, the earth revolving, orbit thrown across the sky. Yesterday Gen had left another country. How could it be? She has travelled with the sun. It seems she can not stop travelling; her mind rushes through the events of the day even as her body lies on the futon, the thick mofu. The night is cool with a fading chill of winter. Gen turns, restless. In stillness she can hear a clanging train bell, rushing darkness. From the Shinkansen at Shizuoka they had taken the donko to Shimizu and from there a taxi. Gen had sat back as the Kintetsu man drove through the narrow roads with his immaculate white gloves, the automatic click of the meter marking passage.

They pulled into the lane and everything changed, the road cutting into where the shed should have been. Bachan must have seen it, the surprise on Gen's face for she smiled, nudging her gently, "O-kaerinasai, Urashima Taro."

O-kaerinasai. Yes, she had come home.

Bowing across the threshold. Here. Tadaima.

Gen burns the incense, pours water over the stone. She had placed her father's ashes in her grandmother's hands. Bachan's hands were wrinkled and shrivelled, spotted but still very strong. They walked across the village, Gen taking in the new pachinko palace, an Apita depato replacing Yoshinori's hatake. Bachan in her wide brim hat stopped ever so often, catching her breath in the shade. Jizo stood by the entrance in straw hat, red bib, a hand holding salvation as easily as the pink Hamamatsu peaches in the machi. They passed stone upon stone, carved names, ancient incantations. Bachan stopping, pointing out friends, neighbours, distant kin. Gen traced the ancient stone, worn smooth by rain. Bachan lights a bundle of green incense, smoke curling above her head. *Namuamidabutsu, namuamidabutsu.* Gen watches. Clasped hands, prayer. How does it feel to bury your only child, beloved son, to burn incense in his name? He has come back to you, come back to this. Looking around her Gen wonders how he ever could have left. Here the stones face the ocean. The mountain towers above them, sloping into bamboo groves. Wind. But life had been different after the war. A widow with a young child, Bachan had sent him to relatives in the city. She lost him even then. How hard it had been, Gen never asked and Bachan never told her.

Gen places her hands together, whispering a prayer. Turning, she catches Bachan's eye.

"Ma, otosan ni yoku niteru. Sokkuri."

Gen opens her mouth, her throat dry.

Bachan shakes her head, her voice low, resigned. "Ah Kenji, muzukashi kodomo datta ne." She slowly walks out of the yard, into sunlight and shadow.

They take supper, a banquet of unagi, amaiebi, sushi, manju, and casadera, their feet tucked into the warmth of the kotatsu. Gen notes that Bachan has no central heating, thinks of the depato, for a present of electric blanket, mofu. And after dinner, they walk to the neighbourhood ofuroya. Scrubbing the backs of women, ricochet chatter, soaking in a rush of heat, an uncomplicated nakedness.

They steep in the public bath, cleansing heat, the slap of water and tile. Bachan asks of her life, that distant land of cold and perhaps a kekkonshiki?

Gen shakes her head, smiling.

"Demo, samishiku nai?" Bachan asks, you aren't lonely?

Gen explains, I'm my own person, Bachan. She straightens as the water laps against her chin.

"Masaka!" Young people today. Who will take care of you when you're old, Bachan shakes her head.

Gen, who knows, if anything, that there are no guarantees, remains silent. She sits back, water over her shoulders, mist rising, and closes her eyes. Thinks of the stone shrine, offerings of incense and oranges.

But "Yononakani... wakara nai ne," Bachan reflects. I just want you to be happy, she sighs, "kokoro ni."

In your heart.

Kokoro, a simple word, with so many meanings. Gen nods over the rising steam.

"Mah, ne."

Bachan grasps with a trembling hand, and Gen sees seventy-two years in her face, her eyes. In the change room, as they dress, Gen muses at the rituals of everyday life, she steps in, a stranger, the ties of blood, across years and language. Obachan, she wonders, what am I to Bachan? Why, why am I here?

But on their way home, gazing into the sky, Bachan points: Look, there are rabbits on the moon.

And so there are.

After Bachan sets out the mofu for the night, she returns with a simple white envelope and places it in Gen's hands. Gen gently pushes it back, thinking of the small pension, the worn yukata wrapped around her grandmother's small frame. "Bachan, tondemonai —"

To Gen's surprise Bachan takes the envelope, spilling the contents onto the table.

A necklace, a letter, a flutter of paper cranes and some faded photographs.

It's all I have of her, Bachan murmurs, your mother.

Gen caresses the fragile thread of silver in her hands as it slips through her fingers like sand, caught, like the rustle of brittle leaves.

"Sachiko," Bachan sighs. Look, you have her eyes. A girl in her school uniform, a young woman, really. A photograph smaller than the palm of your hand. Charred edges. Her family died in the war, in Yokohama, Bachan explains, "bakudan." Faded yellow, a young woman and an older man, standing with a child, Sachiko as a child. Fire. Do you understand, Bachan asks. Your grandparents.

Gen nods. "Okasan."

Bachan pushes open the sliding doors, the train clangs across the fields, the moon low in the sky.

She sets out early in the day, to the Maruki Bijutsukan, to see the Hiroshima murals. From Tokyo station she takes the denshya line north into the prefecture of Saitama and from the station, takes a taxi, a long taxi drive through the inaka, the fields, trees, slips of bamboo, green to the end of the drive, to a house, which is ordinary enough, a house that is also a gallery.

Quiet, so quiet. She steps across the threshold.

It takes a moment, the adjustment of her iris and light. Afterwards, Gen cannot recall what she saw first, but she remembers the size, the colour, the feel of her neck craning up, her legs tensing, breath shallow. Ghosts. Water. Fire. The faces, so many, and nameless. The murals of Hiroshima. A painting, a lantern, a light.

Nanking. Nagasaki.

Human figures, the wash of sumi-e, colour, space, emptiness... why did they paint this horror? She walks alone through this space, this calm and quiet hall, framed by horrors, the caves of Okinawa, the prisoners of Auschwitz, thinking, do they have faces? And eyes? Their stories, mute against the panels, whisper in the trace of ink and brush. Could it be their names?

She stops in front of the mural, the Rape of Nanking, the image of a young girl, braids twisting into ropes, arms bound. In Hiroshima, the rag doll in the wasteland, the rainbow. The distorted faces of children in Minamata. Step back, and back, the murals loom above.

She sees a tablet, inscribed:

Crows
Koreans and Japanese look alike
In those mercilessly charred faces
*   how can one see a difference?*

"After the Bomb, the bodies of the Koreans
were left on the streets to the very last.
Some were alive but few. Nothing to be done.

Crows descending from the sky. Hordes of crows.
Coming down to eat the eyes of the Koreans.
Eat the eyes."

Even in death, Koreans were discriminated against
Even in death, Japanese discriminated against Koreans
Asians both, hit by the Bomb.

Lesbians v,
Heterosexuals?

Beautiful chima chogori
Flying through the sky to Korea
the homeland
We respectfully offer this painting
We pray

Some five thousand Koreans died together in Nagasaki, where they had
been brought as forced labour for the Mitsubishi shipyards. There are
similar stories about Koreans in Hiroshima.

Nearly fifteen thousand atomic bomb survivors live in Korea today.

She steps back and stands before a mural of swirling greys, red
bleeding black into darkness. Jigoku. There, they are there, Toshi
and Iri Maruki, in this vision of hell, falling, falling. There with the
ghosts, the tyrants, the murderers. They painted themselves into these
panels, here with the dying, the living and the perpetually damned.
    Faces. They follow us with their eyes.

She steps through the doors, wind on her hands, sees the riverbank
below, the schoolgirls in their yellow caps dancing like wildflowers by
the stream.

At noon she takes the train north, to Hanaoka, to the old community
hall. She walks among the tall pine trees, the dark and stoney earth.
She searches for a plaque, a stone, any memorial. She does not find it.

By the stone shrines on the mountainside, Gen holds a handful of paper cranes. She gazes into the evening sky, the ceaseless motions of a wine-dark sea. From here she could imagine it, darkness shrouding a western shore. Gen turns towards the entrance, Jizo by the fountain, and sees her standing there.

"Bachan?"

"Sa," Bachan exclaims, as she slowly made her way to Gen's side, I thought you would be here. "Bijutsukan wo mimashita?"

Gen nods.

Bachan turns to face the ocean, the endless expanse of sky. She roots in her pocket and pulls out a pouch, offering a napkin folded over three white balls of rice: onigiri. Gen smiles. Offerings, and here, what can you give. Looking over the rain-worn stone, she thinks of the ocean below. How little time for them to become the sea-washed sands. So much grief between. And the murals, a strange chronicle of horrors. In Nanking the Japanese army killed more people than were killed in Hiroshima and Nagasaki combined. But that image: a doll in the inferno. There are so many faces. What are their names? Do you wonder, in hell, is it our complicity or our helplessness?

Mercy, she thinks. Jizo at the crossroads, arms folded, sleeves holding the souls of lost children for the journey across the river.

Gen steps out, over the promontory. But I am not my father, all over again. She stands, between the mountains and the sea.

Kokoro.

On the last day, Bachan sets out a feast of broiled eels and rice. She places her gifts in a square cloth, wrapped to form a bundle. The takuhaibin have taken Gen's luggage, she is set to leave. Bachan has arranged a game of gate ball and they agree to part ways, not by the station, but by the green lawn of the city park.

It is the last day, Gen reminds herself, thinking of all the questions she had for Bachan. Yet she holds back, uncertain. She thinks of the murals, the silence of the hall. Gen shakes herself. Here, as the women stand in their broad hats, the wooden balls rolling on the green. Bachan. Take a photograph. Gen smiles into the light. It is the only thing she can remember.

Through the glass corridor, partitions of steel, Gen traverses the mirroring doors, to the rumble of the plane. She sits by the window, looking along the concrete runway, what was once fields, now Narita Kuko. What was once a rural landscape paved now with machines of flight. They take you away, take you away. But then, Gen reflects, they had fought it, the farmers, and fight it still. Yet where will she hear about it? Romantic visions of homelands were illusions after all. But we choose. Between heaven and hell? Gen is not so sure. She thinks of the prostitutes in the port cities, mostly Thai and Filipino women and the 'comfort women' of World War Two. Gen turns from the window. Complicity or helplessness. Karasu. What the world will never know.

I am going home.

Turning, below her, Chiba-ken, patchwork of green, turning away, away. Home. Father's ashes, mother's bones. Daibutsu, Hello Kitty, Jizo, unagi. I take you back, take you back. Mother's sorrow, father's shame. I am myself, after all, after everything. Bachan with her incense and Gen with her prayer beads, turning east against the sun.

Snapshot Eye

Imprint on retina.

Gen Tanaka wakes. Her cup slaps across the table as she jerks away. Not her apartment, the stacked boxes, the sleeping bag on futon. She sits, surrounded by an odd geometry of projector, reels. Plop, plop of her coffee, dribbling to the floor. Gen peels herself off the duct tape couch, the smell of rancid butter and popcorn wafting through the rattling vent. Her irises contract to the square patch of window, cutting through the space of the room, a sudden depth, perspective. Gen knows the properties of light, how light holds prisms, can bend to forces greater than gravity. She blinks and pushes open the door, strides down the balcony aisle. Her feet stick, stick, for a moment, to the theatre floor.

"Gen. Gen." Chelsea calls from the first floor.

Gen stumbles down the fading plush carpet, down the spiralling staircase, a throwback to the theatre's vaudeville days. She quickly passes the posters of *Casablanca* and *Citizen Kane*, but it is at *Un Chien andalou* and *Les Yeux sans visage* that her fingers tap against the wooden rail. At the bottom of the stairwell her glance cuts to the fungal wall stain, sweating pipes, the flaking dandruff of the ceiling.

At the concession counter Fed-Ex Stan twirls a stick of black licorice, his clipboard jutting out, the film cans tumbled at his feet. "Sign." He offers his bic, twisted by his restless jaws, but Gen shakes her head, scans the board, drawing a pen out of her pocket.

"What's it going to be tonight?" Chelsea leans over the chocolate bars, crushing the peanut butter cups, "Fellini again?"

Gen scratches the clipboard. "No. *Hiroshima, mon amour.* Don't you ever read the schedule?" She hands back the board. "Thanks Stan."

Stan shrugs and shuffles out the door with Chelsea gazing after him.

"For Christ sake Chelsea, ask him out."

"Nah," Chelsea stacks the chocolate bars, cracking her gum, "I'd never trust a man in a uniform."

At Dooney's Gen watches the street stroll by, the flora and fauna of the west Bloor Annex, a mix of gothic and grunge, backpack, briefcase, buttons like *Free Leonard Peltier* and *No Blood for Oil.* She tracks to the bikes cluttering the walk, chained to posts, trees, even to a black labrador sprawling by the door. Gen cups her coffee in her hands, closes her eyes, opens them, sees the city in snapshots, through the filter of afternoon light.

"Gen, Gen."

She opens her eyes.

Naomi Chiba stands beside her, her sax strap dangling. "So, how's it going?"

Chibi chiba, Gen thinks, small as her name and twice as fast. She blinks, pulls back and away.

"I haven't seen you in a while."

Gen shrugs. "I've just been taking some space."

"Some space?" Nao smiles. "Feels like the Gulf of Mexico to me."

Gen lifts and sets her cup, lifts and sets, the liquid O, a punctuation.

"Some girls at AL are getting together for some basketball down on Church, wanna try and check it out? The shorter you are, the better."

Gen shakes her head.

"Well, can't say I haven't tried." Naomi twists her napkin. She holds her words, exhales them. "Kathy's worried about you."

"I can't do anything about that."

"Get over yourself, Gen."

"What?"

"She doesn't owe you anything."

Gen leans forward, pushing her table, her cup overturned. "You don't either. So why don't you just stay out of this?"

"Just don't screw yourself."

"Fuck off." Gen rises, shoves the chair aside. "And I'm not the one to talk to, remember? My ass got kicked out, not hers."

"Yeah? I guess it depends on how you see it."

Gen walks to the door, pushing through. On the sidewalk she glances at the black dog, the posts covered with leaflets. She gazes down the street, a long take of the afternoon unravelling, the sun eclipsed by the trees.

In the projection booth, Gen throws the film cans on the table, chewing on a Snickers bar. She takes the reel from *Hiroshima*, threads the leader through the projector, into sprocket, loop, then shutter, snaking into the other reel. The cla cla claclacla of the turning spools, as she pulls focus, the rolling frame slipping, then caught, into the wheels of the apparatus. Apparatus, she thinks, this nineteenth century machine of spinning clicks and revolving whirls. She throws the lights into darkness. And waits.

Hiroshima begins with the city. Seven rivers, a map of an impossible world. Here, the atomic museum, the story of the film and of the film within the film, the flicker of image, the persistence of vision. Gen has seen this film over and over, can never remember the ending, does she leave him, this city, does she forget? What does she see, this woman? Gen kills the lamp, rewinds to the beginning, cla cla cla in the dark.

The eye is a camera, Gen knows, but the optic nerve is blind.

On the spiral staircase, as she munches on her Snickers bar, Gen stumbles, catching herself on the rail. Snap of jaw, and tooth, she feels it swimming in its pocket, tastes the rusty iron, sour. In the washroom, with a handful of rough paper towels, she wipes the blood from her lips. She opens her mouth, spits, rinses, peering closer. At the back, a molar, her tongue flicking against an odd rubbing, a pool of pink saliva. Gen rocks back in surprise: the tooth, in its cavity, has split right in half, no pain, but a shivering fascination of a torn fingernail, crusty scab pulling away. I am falling apart, Gen thinks, and smiles ghoulish in the mirror.

"What the hell happened?" Chelsea demands, staring at Gen's bloody mouth as she strides out of the washroom.

Gen hands her the Snicker's wrapper. "Busted my damn tooth on one of your damn candy bars. How old are they anyway?"

"Carper deum."

Gen laughs. "That's caveat emptor, Chel." She takes her jacket from behind the concession stand. "Was that clinic down on Spadina? Don't worry, I'll be back by six."

In the waiting room of the Spadina Dental Clinic, Gen flips through the year-old magazines. She has filled out the requisite forms and waivers and sits with a wad of toilet paper stuffed in her mouth. Above her the plastic mobile of Mister Mouth and Missus Molar click and clatter. The gigantic poster of Tooth Decay, rot blackened teeth and all, glowers from the wall. Gen, who used the last of her dental floss to string popcorn for the winter solstice, cringes at the sight. Beside her, on the table, there is a model of a dissected head, the severed corpus callumus, an eyeball, half a nose, teeth rattling in sockets. Nudge and the brain unravels like stiff intestines. An eyeball rolls to the floor.

"Ms. Tanaka," the receptionist calls.

Gen rises.

The receptionist smiles, directs her into a brightly sterile room, a padded pale blue chair. "Dr. Barker will be right with you."

The window in the office faces north, and from her seat Gen can see Jule's co-op and the Native Friendship Centre to her right, the houses on Brunswick to her left, shaded by large oaks and maples. Gen takes the toilet paper out of her mouth, spits into the rinser. She leans back, staring into the distended eye of the overhead lamp, bounces up, clicking the sections of her tooth together, the squish-squirt of saliva held in her mouth. On the walls, a row of x-rays, skeletal, phantom-white. Restless she walks to the window, envisions an escape to five stories down. She leans forward and the blinds ripple, light waves, steel and glass.

"Hello. Gen Tanaka." Dr. Barker is reading off his sheet. He is a middle-aged white man, hands encased in latex. His mustache is neat, smile friendly, his dark hair peppered with grey. "Please sit down. What seems to be the problem?"

"My tooth — "

"Ah," the doctor swings the overhead lamp, "let's take a look, shall we?"

Gen opens her mouth, "At the back." Her tongue flicks the crack, the fissure opens and Dr. Barker is visibly taken aback.

"My, it's split right in half." He probes the tooth. "Yes, it has got to come out, it's split down to below the gumline. Sorry, it can't be saved." Barker folds his hands. "Do you have any insurance?"

Gen shakes her head.

"Well, you're going to need a bridge, maybe not right away, but soon."

"Hm. How much would that be?"

Dr. Barker takes a breath. "Fifteen hundred, at the least."

"Fifteen hundred?"

"Yes." Barker sat back. "I know it's quite a hefty sum."

Gen bites her lip. "Can I pass on it. I mean, it's not urgent, or anything, is it?"

"Well, you'll have to have that bridge put in, or your teeth'll be really messed. Teeth are serious business. They have to hold out for the rest of your life, and you, you're still young. I'll tell you what. I'll pull this out, no charge, and maybe by the time you need the bridge, your job'll have it covered, or you'll have some kind of insurance. Maybe hit up the folks for some kind of plan. You can leave it for a year, two at the tops, but no more, or your teeth'll start moving around. Okay?"

Gen blinks. "Thank you." She has a sudden urge to shake his hand.

He smiles, Dr. Barker, meets her eyes. "Hey, I've been there." He pushes the lamp down. "They don't call this a recession for nothing."

In the washroom, they stand by the sink. "So how was it?" Chelsea leans forward. She stares, not at Gen, but her reflection.

"Like poolling teece." Gen spits into the sink. Her jaw is frozen and a pinkish drool collects beneath her tongue. She spits again and inspects the red gaping hole. She opens her fist and holds in her palm two hard, sharp stones, pale yellow. Her tooth, broken in half. She rattles the pieces.

"Wow, they're just like bone." Chelsea picks up the sections of the tooth, places them together. "My God, it's huge, I'm surprised it even fit in your mouth." She peers at Gen's forehead. "What's that?"

"Wha?"

"What's that on your forehead?"

Gen gazes in the mirror. "Oh. Brooth. Thepped on an eyeball." She unwraps the gauze from her pocket.

"Hm." A sidewards glance and Chelsea reaches into her purse, "I've got something... it'll pickle your gums." Pulls out a mickey of Snakebite, *33% proof* in small print beneath of the logo of a flaming red Cobra. "Disinfectant," she explains.

Gen looks up, her face owlish in surprise.

"It's for emergencies, okay?"

"Thanths."

"Well, you gotta have someone looking out for you."

"I'm not that helpleth."

"How many people step on eyeballs, okay? Have to admit, Kathy took care of you. And she's so sweet, I just can't believe — hey —"

But Gen is out the door.

In the projection booth she takes a swig of whiskey, holds it in her frozen mouth, tasting nothing, swallows. She feels the fast burn down her throat, a glow in the pit of her stomach. Below her, the theatre slowly fills by twos and threes, with the occasional solitary spectator. Gen holds the bottle, dims the lights, and from behind the thick glass and soundproof walls, starts the clattering machine, the lamp, the sprockets, loops and reels. Her cheeks flush as the liquid burns in her veins. She takes off her glasses, sees the screen without focus and thinks of eyes, of how the image is inverted, aqueous fluid, as she drinks another searing drink, thinking of how light can blind, of coronas and ellipsis, of the eye that sees what is not there, the cla cla claclacla string of images and shadow, the spinning reels of *Hiroshima*, whose eyes behind the camera, she wonders, whose story of forgetting?

Gen stares at the black and white screen, her thoughts cut into memory; Kathy — a photograph, she is young, a wine glass in her hand, hair cut shoulder length, and alone. The summer of her father's dying. But photographs are forever lying, a presentness of past imperfect. Lies. Kathy and Gen smiling at the camera, snapshot; given time, all your hopes betray you. Gen wipes the image from her mind. She stumbles, the bottle empty. Films have cells, a ribbon of nucleic acid, sprockets like rockets, an absence, like the heart. She is drunk, drunk and stinking, her lost tooth in her hand. She sits back, the story unravelling, her eyes closed. Curtain.

Fade.

She wakes, the projector still rolling, slap, slap of film slipping from revolving reel. The lights in the theatre are up, shining into the booth, the yellow warmth of tungsten.

She clicks off the apparatus, leaving the strip of film hanging from the wheel and staggers down the staircase, vertigo. In the foyer she sees Chelsea with her cash sheet and waves an uncertain goodbye as she rushes out the door. She huddles through the late night crowd. Her skin feels taut, cannot bear a touch, a falling glance. At the subway she takes out her wallet, a glick-ching as her token falls through, and a push through the revolving wheel, spat out to the platform, momentum, a mechanical force, like a ball in a Goldberg machine.

Jump to subway car, Gen nods, the noodle-neck subway syndrome, stop-jerk of motion, the eyes shutter close, station reels away. Jerk-snap-waking, passed her stop, but stays on, catch the loop, catch the loop around... Missed stop miss stop missstop misstopmistop — Gen darts out at Broadway, bursts to the surface, realizing she's on the other side of the bridge. Cool air, streetcar clang clang. She begins walking across the ondaatje bridge she calls it, above the weakly flowing Don.

Wind strong. She spits into the darkness.

Her tongue flicks to the gap in her mouth and she thinks of Dr. Barker. "A nith man," Gen says, and thinks of Chelsea, Nao and Kathy, all nice. And I, Gen wonders. No. I am not nice. Not nice. All in the way you see it, Nao had said. Gen heaves bile, swallows it. Her insides feel hollow.

She stops at Castle Frank.

Across the bridge, the other direction she reminds herself, a short cut through St. James. She squeezes through the gap in the spiked fence, stumbles on the stone in the grass. Up. The sky is lighter through the trees. Passing the gravestones, onto the gravel path, the wind stirring up branches, leaves. Shhh. Listen. Gen stops, hears the footsteps, turns. "Whoooce sare?" Squirrels scuttling across the bark of oak trees. Hm. But Gen knows better.

Gen steps off the path, down the hill, runs to a growing momentum. She can feel the hot breath of the other, can hear the footsteps fall closer, closer. She stops to turn, but the centre is off and Gen, falling.

Blink, blink, as she opens her eyes. And sees the stranger, towering above her. Light, dim from the distant street, but enough to make out a smooth rain-worn head, two inexplicable stubs on the back, stone crumbling. Gen peers.

"Jizo — "

Of course, Gen thinks. She stands, dusts off. The world is spinning less, the stars hold the universe in place. She turns. She can see the gap in the wall. And up, the moon has risen.

She looks over the graveyard. Quiet. Jizo has not said a word. The wind, rustling the leaves. Gen shivers. Thinks, must be cold, the nights, even now.

Jizo, standing. Waiting.

Gen takes off her jacket, drapes it over the stone shoulders. From her pocket, she takes her cap, sets it on the round stone head. She steps back, walks to the gap, waves, walks on to Winchester, down Parliament, walking home. At the doorstep she jingles the knob, fumbles with the keys.

Light. Blink, blink.

The door opens, and Kathy stands in surprise but Gen, in greater surprise. Wrong house, not her new apartment but old, familiar home, but no, lips wet, as her hand brushes away, explaining, "Toooccee..."

She leans forward, sick on Kathy's new slippers.

Fade.

Truce, you've called it, Kathy sighs, and was it so hard, after all, after everything. She pulls the sheets around Gen, asleep in the bed. Kathy strokes the maru-maru head, short bristling hair, a bruise from a rolling eyeball. Behind her stands the small stone statue of Jizo, head bowed, hands clasped, praying by the window.

Pomegranates and Pomelos

They are stranded, Aiko, Masao and Kaori between them, her legs spread to catch them if they should slip between the gaps of the chair. At this height they can see across the reservoir, to Glenmore Trail, maybe even to the jagged edge of Kananaskis, or the bristled ridge of the Porcupines. Kaori does not look, does not even try; she's stuck on the ancient ferris wheel at Heritage park while the two teenagers (conductors? Kaori wonders, attendants?) bicker and snipe. How long have they been fighting? The ride does seem interminably long. Kaori bites her lip, tries not to swing the chair. She does not like heights, this precarious stillness. Aiko and Masao sit in silence after the cotton candy and merry-go-round, their fingers sticky, and lips, halos of unnatural blue and green. Blue for Aiko, green for Masao — at three and seven, they fight even over colours. Their eyes are drowsy in the gentle swing of chair, suspension, without floating care. But Kaori looks down, cautiously shifts her centre of gravity. Below, Setsuko waves, smiling. A flare of anger as Kaori steams — fool, fool, get me down from here, don't you see the danger, no, never you — but to shout would rock the chair so her rage rolls off and over.

The light of the late afternoon is strong, prickles her skin, she feels the heat run up her arm, along her shoulders, down the bridge of her nose; they hang exposed, Kaori realizes, without the shield of sunscreen. Television newsreels spin through her head — *American Rescues* and *Disaster 911*. But there is no commotion, no panic, not a video camera in sight.

Kaori sits back. Stuck on a ferris wheel. She wills herself to unclench the safety bar. Her nails are bitten to the bone. Unnerving, she thinks, this waiting, nothing to do. At home, her annual reports fester in her briefcase, venn diagrams and graphs that hold days, months, even years. File by Monday, meeting on Tuesday, seed account, inventory, p.d.q. As she taps her feet together twenty metres above the ground, she thinks, high and dry, no place like home. She glances down at the quarrelling teenagers (operators? drivers?). Are they friends? Lovers? These two young men, boys really, with their *Just Do Me* t-shirts and baseball caps. She looks at the crowd below. She's so small, Kaori realizes, Setsuko looks so small. Why even gravity could crush her.

Kaori lifts her legs, feels the suspension of the chair — swings — if only by millimetres, clutches the safety bar. The sun feels close against her skin. She remembers pomegranates in this heat, bite of seed-pebbles in her mouth, red, the thick skin of pomelos, opening like starfish, blood oranges in chinatown boxes, the crunch of square persimmons. Kaori stares at the sky, where prairies bleed into foothills, coulees into valleys, and she thinks that birds must fly against this blue, scraping against dust and stone. A sky to bury you, she murmurs, blue, azure, indigo.

The wheel jolts as it rolls one seat forward, then glides towards landfall, halts as the safety bar rises and Kaori, Masao and Aiko step off the ferris wheel, legs on solid ground.

They run down the ramp, Masao and Aiko squealing.

Whew, Kaori brushes back her hair, her fingers stiff from gripping the bar. Do you know how long we were stuck up there?

Stuck? Setsu shakes her head, glancing back at the wheel. I didn't even notice. Are you sure?

Yes! We must have been. The ride just took forever.

Setsuko laughs.

What?

You just don't have any patience, Setsuko replies, shaking her head. They have to let everyone off, one by one.

What?

But Setsuko is laughing, holding the hands of her sticky children and Kaori can only smile. Damn right I don't have any patience! Come on, last one to the gates is a rotten egg.

Off they run, Kaori, Masao and Aiko, with Setsuko trailing after.

Driftwood

Dreaming of rain, but no, the wind lashing against glass. Norma Nakashima sits up in the bed, shadows strange, this room, unfamiliar. Her hand on the lamp, light filling spaces of chair, desk, window. Her hotel room in Vancouver. She slips out of the bed and walks to the window, brushing aside the heavy curtains. Sprinkle of lights along Burrard Inlet, up to Grouse Mountain. Norma thinks of Robbie, asleep now, or maybe chewing through one of her duty casseroles. Or Kathy, who had driven up the weekend before with Gen, full of confusion and blustering worry. Norma sighs and slips back between her bleach scented sheets.

In the morning Norma rises, forsakes the hotel's Bounty Breakfast. She walks down to the east end, through streets of glitter and glass, enclaves of steel. Her feet click clack through the cobblestone of Gastown. At Powell, her voice begins to rework the landscape. Nakano's shop, Ohashi's tree, Jay and Barbara's garden. The clothesline that ran from the Kitagawa's to Ito-san, the fight at the brothel on Alexander, stories of 1907, the

\ 95

riots and rumours, boarding house gamblers and newly-arrived brides. Along Princess, around Cordova. Until an empty lot, strewn with scraps of lumber, the twisting shells of abandoned automobiles, she stops, points. "Here," she murmurs, "our house was here."

Norma glances up. No, there is no one around. But she is muttering to herself like a crazy old woman. She clucks her tongue. Chickens coming home to roost. But she steps into Furusato for some manju. Time, she still has time before heading out to Richmond, the reception. Michiko, she hasn't seen Michiko in almost fifty years. How did Michiko find her? And why, why had she come?

Norma sits on the bench at Oppenheimer Park, gazes at the mountains, the strangeness of such grasping elevation. But Vancouver, the mountains and the bay, so familiar, and green, monkey tails and moss on the trees. She thinks of the joke from the man beside her on the plane. Hongcouver, he said. What did he mean, she wonders. She sees the ramshackle state of the block, a street person's claim of a corner, the huddle by a table, the bottles by the crate. Other kinds of homes.

Norma turns her head. A sweet smell of burning.

At the corner of the park, at the baseball diamond, she can see a small gathering of First Nations women. Indians, she thinks. There've always been Indians on Powell Street. Curious, she walks towards them. A woman, tall, brown hair cropped short, is tying ribbons to the steel mesh of the diamond. Ribbons marked with names. Norma can barely make them out before they are snatched by the wind. The women form a circle and she can hear the murmur of voices, sometimes one, sometimes many. Norma hangs back, behind the fence, unwilling to intrude into a story where she does not belong. She turns, can see Grouse Mountain dusted by cloud.

Michiko, she thinks.

Jan breaks the circle, her hand runs across the bristles of her hair. The streaming ribbons, fifteen names of Native women killed on the streets in the east end. What had Lise said? Their names becoming 'a poem of our lives.' More than were given by the damn cops, Kelly had said, bitterly. Jan looks up at the tendrils of red, yellow, green. Scratched into the pole, "Five hundred years and counting." She pours the water from her bottle on the ground, an offering, a cleansing, and she has a sudden image of dragonflies, the crystal sliver of wings. She waves, calls out to the women of the circle, and Lise, Lise runs up with a rough kiss as they walk to the car. Jan looks back as Lise pulls up Jackson in the rusting Tercel. Along Hastings she can see Yuriko's murals on the side of the warehouse, the graffiti on Venables: *Oka is still all of us.*

Jan sits on her balcony off Commercial. To her right she can see the sign of the Cuervos co-op, can hear Mercedes singing gracias to life, the only words of Spanish Jan really knows. Behind her, with her back to the window, Lise sits at her computer, mutters and whispers to the screen. Jan turns her head, as if to catch the falling phrases, but she can only hear click of the keyboard, an occasional, abandoned word. When Lise works, Jan sits on the balcony, away from the rituals that Lise creates around her. Lise who always writes in the limited omniscient because she "doesn't do well in the first person." Lise, the writer, drops into her separateness, her faith in words, where a poem can fall from wheatbread, scatter out of spiralling bird wings.

Jan peels the label off her beer, rolls the bits between her fingers. West, she can see the skyline, maybe even the ocean in the fading light. Jan checks her watch, the length of shadow against the moss covered brick. She rises and slides the keys off the kitchen table. She glances back: Lise at her computer, blue screen reflected in her eyes. Softly Jan closes the door behind her, skips down the stairs, two at a time. She takes the route through Denman to English Bay, parks the car near the bridge and walks along the crest of the slope down to the beach. Until now, Jan has never lived near the sea, but feels a strange elation at the push and retreat, the ceaseless motion. She stares at the vastness of the water, tastes the edge of salt in her lungs. Even the ships in the bay look like massive lonely creatures, as the light slips through the cracks of the mountains, shadows long against the horizon's curve. Jan walks to the edge, the water licking her shoes and whispers, I would give anything to sing, to swim. She thinks of Lise and she wants to fly.

She turns and waits, sees a woman down by the rocks. Jan picks her way back along the slope, to the bridge, back to her car. Lise may have dinner on the stove: one of the unexpected benefits of writer's block. Jan turns, gazes at the fading light. The islands are distant, the mountains, clear. She turns the ignition and heads home.

Norma walks along the shoreline, her shoes in her hand. The wedding and reception are long over. She even caught the bouquet. She has seen Michiko and her now-husband, Dennis Bouganville and knows that Michiko had gotten her address from the NAJC, Ottawa chapter, for the invitation. She knows that after the war, the dispersal, Michiko had searched for her, to no avail. Why, Norma did not ask. Norma's heels sink in the wet sand and she has cold fish feet; the grains rub between her toes. Michiko's face is older, but she still has the face of an imp, a troublemaker — and her first marriage at sixty-two. Her hair is a silvered gray, and her eyes, a lighter, clearer brown. But what Norma remembers is a cellar of salted salmon, cool in the summertime of her childhood, the scent of peppermints on her breath. Michiko is there, in pink floral dress and they are hiding from the older ones, brothers and sisters, under the stairs in Norma's cellar. Norma, whose name is still Harumi Watanabe, before the journey, the boxes and departures, before the war.

But the peppermints.

Michiko is smiling, a gleaming white candy on her tongue, in her mouth, on her lips. Here, gone, here, gone. Click, click, against her teeth.

The breath of peppermints.

Click, click. Tongue, mouth, lips.

Harumi leans forward, sucks the peppermint off Michiko's lips, sweet and cool — the electric shiver of tongue and tongue.

Norma remembers. Has she ever forgotten? What does it matter? She steps out to the rocks, throws the bouquet to the tide. A splash and the flowers bob, then slowly they are pulled out to sea.

mother + daughter really aren't that far apart

why the problems of silence?

Stone
Heart

Riding along University, as her small black bicycle darts alongside the belligerent cars, Gen takes in the wreathed memorials, hearts of stone and steel. A red light on Dundas, and she waits beside a statue nicknamed Gumby Goes to Heaven. Gen shoves back her gloves, bitten off at the tips. She shivers, places her foot down on the curb. Five years ago Sami was arrested for placing a banner on the monument on Queen Street, a banner in remembrance of the women and children maimed, raped and killed by the Unknown Soldier. Remembrance Day, Gen sighs, and what do we remember in this culture of amnesia? Dying, would they have chosen this, those soldiers, engraved in cold, cold stone? Gen grips her handbars, her fingers numb. Alone, she feels the icy chill of a gray November day. She slaps her thighs as the light turns green and pushes off into the traffic.

Outside the 519, she locks up her bike and shuffles up the stairs. It was in this building that Gen huddled, nearly a year ago, waiting for the end of the world; scud missiles, warheads, biological weapons and terrorist/counter-terrorist armageddons. But it had not happened, or, as Gen reminded herself, it had not happened to her. And what could poetry do? A hundred fifty thousand killed in a war flashing on the screens like video games. Where were the faces, the eyes — their murals and photographs? What good is a poet against grief? There are no words to contain it. Amidst the rumours of nuclear deterrents and internment, the double-speak of "smart bombs" and "collateral damage" and a media campaign of bread and circuses. There had been demonstrations, sit-ins, placards raised, pamphlets spread, the cries of, "No blood for oil." Yet here she is, yet again. Strange, Gen reflects, how you expect the big, historic moments in a life to leap out, to drag you from dimness into searing light, to carve you into witness, like a face in a photograph. Do we remember, or do we continually forget? At the doorway, Gen sees Naomi scurrying about the podium with her tape recorder, she remembers that Clara is in the refugee camps near San Cristobal, organizing the return to a country which has few political prisoners, because they are dead.

She pushes through the crowd, into the auditorium. Her gaze sweeps over the seats, to the banners hanging on the walls: *Freedom for Peltier, Garment Workers for Justice, Women Working Against Violence. Memorial:* November 11, 1992 and Audre Lorde is dead.

The crowd stirs as Lisa stands at the podium. Kathy's friend, Lisa Compton. Gen scans the room, returning to the tall Black woman on the stage. Lisa, who heads the Toronto Coalition Against Racist Policing. She adjusts the mic as the crowd settles. Her voice is low and steady as she begins to read "For Each of You" from Lorde's *Chosen Poems.*

Surrounded by a stack of books Naomi placed in her care, Gen pulls out a worn copy of *Girls, Visions and Everything*, reads Lila's reflection on the light on the tenement rooftop, of love and belonging, and Gen thinks that love changes you, but not just love, it's more than the books you read, a flutter of pages, more than a smile or a nod on the street. But the women you choose to love. Clara's books, spilling out of Naomi's box, into Gen's hands.

She looks out the window, golden light, the warmth of springtime in November, the vestiges of lost summer.

And Gen shouts that Galeano wrote of joy, how we can't live with hearts of shit, how the machine tries to destroy us, first our hearts, our hopes, so that we can't accept any other world than this, how we need joy, love, to move us to action, that to live means more than survival, that joy is not a crime. And as she traces these lines, Gen, in this light, remembers Cardenal's birds as they flew to the mountain, that even birds have memories, even birds.

Audre Lorde is dead, Gen knows, but her words are in my hands. Gen recalls the story of Buddha guiding a young woman into the deepest pits of hell. What she finds there is a splendid table, a banquet of the most delicious foods, a feast of plenty. Yet at a distance, each person is seated, hands bound, each with an impossibly long fork. It is with this fork that they must feed themselves, fettered as they are. Buddha takes the woman to heaven, yet in heaven there is the same feast, the same clasps, the same impossibly long forks. The young woman asks the Buddha, why then, what is the difference between heaven and hell. The difference. In hell, one feeds oneself, in heaven we feed each other.

The ones that you love. From hand to mouth, these words. An image of Kathy comes to mind, a fallen strand of hair. Gen reflects: I am one who would destroy myself rather than my silences.

The telephone rings shrill, a jangle of wires. Gen snatches the receiver.

"Gen, it's Sandy. Listen, Naomi has gone crazy, she's heading for the airport — she's pawned that damn saxophone — "

"What?"

"She's going to fucking Mexico!"

"I'll be there." Her mind darting, she places the receiver in its cradle. The airport, less than thirty minutes, she grabs her jacket ...

Naomi sits with her chin propped on her arm, surrounded by the electronic buzz of the airport, ricochet calls and murmurings, muffled, distant and opaque. Her flight on standby, she drowses in the stiff plastic seats of the terminal, her bag covers her feet, her head nodding.

"Hey!"

She jolts awake.

Gen.

"What's this I hear about damn Mexico?"

Naomi blinks.

\ 101

"Wake up, buttface."

"I am going to Mexico."

"Clara doesn't need you there."

"But I do."

Gen crosses her arms. "What the hell does that mean? She's coming back. Nao, you've said it yourself, you don't have to do this."

"Yeah, but I can. Don't you see? Because I can."

Gen squints.

"There's work I can do there," Nao continues, "And if it gets too hairy, then I can leave like that," she snaps her fingers, and smiles, wistful, "like the first world baby that I am."

A call, over the address system: "Canada Air Flight 502, to Mexico, boarding at gate 11."

Naomi picks up her bag. "That's me." But Gen's arm holds her back.

"Nao — "

"Don't you see? You were the one who told me. There are no irrevocable moments — never too late, remember? You can't stop me. And Gen, what ever this is, I choose it."

Gen pulls back and glares.

Naomi shakes her head slowly, puts out her hand.

Goodbye.

Gen looks down at the lines on her palm, a hand as small as her own. Chibi Chiba. "Wait," she stammers and runs to the bank machine. A flutter and whirl. She pushes all of her money into Nao's hands, quickly, quickly, emptying her pockets, nickels, dimes, quarters sprinkling the floor. "Go, go, gogogo," almost a shout as she pushes Naomi away, through the glass doors, pushing, until she stands, empty handed.

Flight. A roar. As if to tear open the sky.

She closes her eyes.

It takes her four hours to walk to the lake. At last, crossing the boulevard, down the slope of park, rocky shore to the water, Gen stands, ankle deep. Big beautiful water, the Hurons called it. Rolling, the pull and retreat. Above her the birds circle, wind borne. She smiles, stretching her arms, spinning, in flight of air and water.

Photo: Hiromi Goto

Tamai Kobayashi was born in Japan
and raised in Canada. Her work has
appeared in *absinthe literary journal*,
Fireweed: A Feminist Quarterly, *Piece of
my Heart: A Lesbian of Colour Anthology*
(Sister Vision Press), *Getting Wet: Tales
of Lesbian Seductions* (Women's Press).
She has also coauthored, with Mona
Oikawa, *All Names Spoken* (Sister
Vision Press).